SURFACE PREY

JOHN LEE SCHNEIDER

SEVERED PRESS
HOBART TASMANIA

SURFACE PREY

When that shark bites with his teeth dear, scarlet billows, they begin to spread.

Fancy white gloves though, has Macheath, dear, so there's rarely, never one trace of red.

Mack the Knife.

CHAPTER 1

"The great white shark is not a monster."

As he spoke before the camera, the view panned back to show shark researcher, Stephen Dreyfuss, standing on the rocks overlooking the ocean. In his hands, he was holding a surfboard with a circular bite, approximately two-feet across, taken cleanly out of one corner.

The camera panned in on the bite, then back to Dreyfuss, who was smiling as he stepped aside, giving an open view of the coast.

The Farallon Islands.

The video switched to a helicopter view of the surrounding ocean, and Dreyfuss' own voice narrated a brief history of the local area.

"The Farallons," Dreyfuss intoned in his best professor's voice, "are a chain of islands that lie not thirty miles off the coast of San Francisco. Consisting mostly of large, rocky peaks, the islands are an ideal spot for the seasonal congregations of elephant seals. At the right time of year, the beaches and rocks alike are milling with seals, honking, barking, and fighting and mating – Fort Lauderdale for elephant seals."

The video shifted to a water's eye view of the islands.

"At this time of year, the white sharks are here too."

On camera, the water surface dipped above the camera lens and just below the surface, ascending almost invisibly from the dim blue, was a great white shark.

"These are big ones," Dreyfuss said. "Grown adults."

The scene cut away to clearer views of large sharks – all shot with a camera on a pole from a very small boat – but, as Dreyfuss himself later said, that particular clip was the most effective.

A sudden dip below the surface. And it was already *there.*

It was the third film in Dreyfuss' series, and easily the most popular.

Dreyfuss had produced the first two himself – he was an innovator and, recognizing the white shark's taste for elephant seals, he created a decoy out of a simple surfboard. A camera was attached to the bottom of the board, facing straight down into the water, and reinforced with cement in order to withstand a bite. The board was then dangled out on a thick wire fishing line, out over the rocks.

"It's really just like fishing for trout," Dreyfuss explained. "The shark goes deep, and then comes up from below – just like the movie-poster from JAWS.

"They like surface prey," Dreyfuss says on the video. "A surfboard looks just like the shadow of a seal on the surface."

And the image captured was a head-on view of a great white shark in a full-on attack – often taking both the camera-board and itself fifteen feet clear of the water.

The image was riveting as any filmed in JAWS.

And in interviews, Dreyfuss commented that it was a bit of a moral conundrum.

"I'm a conservationist," he explained, "but it's the scare that sells."

There was, of course, no denying that the scare potential was there. Perhaps he mollified himself by showing the public that the great white was not JAWS – *Carcharodon carcharias* is, in point of fact, a bit unique in that it specifically does *not* tend to eat humans – it is pointedly not the sort of omnivorous garbage-bucket that, say, a tiger shark might be. The truth of the 'man-eater' shark falls somewhat short of the myth.

On the other hand, while real white sharks might not equal JAWS, a sixteen footer is still a very, very large fish. And even though they might not target humans deliberately, they will quite readily strike a likely-looking prey item, particularly if it happens to be on or near the surface.

And being spit out, after the fact, might not be a lot of consolation if you've been bitten in half.

On Dreyfuss' video, an off-camera voice asks, "Would you go swimming in California?"

"Oh sure," Dreyfuss responds. "There are places where it's perfectly safe. The shallows are fine."

Then he hefts his board again, glancing back over his shoulder at the choppy waters of the Farallons.

"Don't get me wrong," Dreyfuss says, with perhaps uncommon candor, as he stares out over the ocean, "I wouldn't go swimming out here for anything."

Which brings us to the story of Colin Mason.

CHAPTER 2

The Farallons don't change. Really, there is no reason why they should, certainly not from the hand of man. They are a nasty, inhospitable bit of coast, interesting only to those who enjoy the harsher things in life, and thus not attracting enough human attention to spoil it. Despite its proximity to the big-city pollution of San Francisco, it remains a largely untouched environment, and a warm August sunset is as beautiful seen from the ocean out on the Farallons as anywhere in the world.

When late afternoon hits, the rugged jetties cast long, reaching shadows, which nearly concealed a large yacht anchored barely a quarter mile beyond the reef. And stretched out on the deck, her beach-oiled body, grasping for the last of the day's sun, Alexis – Alex, to her friends – lay in a pretense of a doze.

Alex pretended to be asleep a lot these days – one of the advantages of traveling on a yacht.

Not that her... sponsor.... cared overmuch what she did in her off-time.

Colin Mason had but one requirement of her, and he had made that quite clear. And Alex – whose real name was 'Laurie' – twenty-one since she was fourteen, blond and LA-pretty, had been part of a regular, comfortable, companion/passenger arrangement with Mason for going on three years now.

And as a whoop sounded from the main cabin, signaling that the party on board the yacht was beginning to get out of hand, Alex thought she had seen it all before.

Mason came back to this spot every year – *why*, Alex wasn't sure. It was the anniversary of his accident; that much she knew - but why that gave him a reason to return was beyond her.

He always called it his 'accident.' And it was the only situation you would ever hear Mason degrade himself. "I was a blind, arrogant fool," he told Alex once. "I deserve to be dead."

Then he had smiled, pushing up against her in bed, his one leg missing, his… equipment… damaged – sometimes it worked, sometimes it didn't – their first time Alex spent nearly an hour with her mouth and hands just getting him started. Afterwards, he had pulled her smooth, nineteen-year-old skin against his grizzled chest and spoke into her ear. "I deserve to be dead," he told her again. "But I learned. And I'm better for it."

And every year he came back here to the Farallons. A celebration? Penance? If asked, Mason himself would have simply said, "The Contest," and left it at that.

A select few of those on the boat tonight were contestants in Mason's Contest.

Most of the rest were hired help.

Colin Mason was the son of a very wealthy businessman who had come into his money during the early days of the Vegas casinos. Showing the rare gambler's ability to quit while ahead, the senior Mason had withdrawn his interests in Vegas mere days before the Federal nets had been officially set, and he had settled comfortably in the younger, more optimistic business-community of the California coast. His visible businesses centered for many years in Real Estate and a brisk trucking and shipping enterprise.

Most of Mason Sr.'s ventures after the seventies were legitimate. In his own words, "The real trick to American business is getting your first stake. Once you've got a large enough pot, you can make money doing anything."

Translation: there was no reason to be outside the law.

Nevertheless, a clandestine reputation followed the Mason clan, and Mason Sr. had maintained a number of old friendships from back east. And when Mason-family business interests occasionally stepped on toes, it was not uncommon for the idealistic opponents of such interests to wind up with broken arms, or turn up missing altogether.

That reputation had only grown since Colin Jr. had taken over.

Whereas Mason Sr. was a working man, Colin Jr. had been born a spoiled prince – and not a kindly one either.

In the beginning, Mason Sr., who had put in seventeen-hour days starting from his eleventh birthday, had frowned on his son's apparently careless hedonistic lifestyle.

He needn't have worried.

Because as Mason himself had once remarked to Alex, what his father failed to see was that Colin Jr.'s penchant for self-indulgence concealed the aggressive drive with which he attacked life. And when the time finally came for the son to take the place of the father, Colin's approach to the family business was a good deal less subtle, but no less effective.

Mason Sr. had come to California basically with retirement on his mind. Colin Jr. was a corporate raider in his prime. And the Mason empire had grown under his watch – as did the shady rumors that followed them.

As such was his life, Colin Mason had few well wishers and less sympathy when, in late August of 1988, he was attacked and nearly killed by a large white shark while scuba diving in the waters off the Farallon Islands.

Giving up on the sun, Alex rose, stretching luxuriously and donning a flimsy robe to cover her nearly-naked body. Stirring her drink casually, she wandered over to rejoin the party in progress in the main cabin.

Mason himself was not yet in attendance. Alex knew the pattern – and the reverence that went with it. In a way, Alex wondered if it was the only way a man like Mason knew how to pray.

It was a ritual. Fourteen years old now.

Alex knew the story well. Mason had told it to her many times.

He even had video.

That was one thing about Colin – the laid-back party image maintained through it all. And perhaps that had been the fatal flaw – the deliberate carelessness that went with it. Never even completing high school, Colin lived on the beach, learned sky diving and sailing, and particularly scuba and surfing.

Colin was an intelligent man, but it could be fairly said that he only became educated where it interested him. In the case of scuba diving, he had learned the mechanics – and had totally blown off any of his instructors' lectures about deceptively academic subjects like ecology. Colin Mason believed in practical matters and had no patience for vague liberal ponderings about the ecology.

It was that very practicality, however, that in the days and weeks of his near-miraculous recovery, lying in the hospital, stitched together like a doll, Colin was forced to accept the fact that it had been his own ignorance that had...

Well..., come back to bite him. So to speak.

If he'd even asked, almost anyone could have told him not to go diving in the Farallons; even in the days before Stephen Dreyfuss' ground-breaking documentaries, the Farallons were known to be a high danger spot. Colin, of course, with his contempt for anything like fear or even simple respect of a power other than his own, had spent most of that day exploring along the rocks. He had, in fact, been musing that the rumors of sharks and seals were overrated – he hadn't seen any seals all day. He had been musing this as he followed his slowest bubble to the top and sat there floating on the surface with a nearly empty tank.

From below, the shadow of a human looks just like a fat little seal.

The shark was estimated as at least a sixteen-footer by the bite marks, and it had typically hit Mason from below – and it had, in fact, been a full-on 'Polaris' attack, as well. There was no bite-and-spit theory employed here; in the waters of the Farallons, thick with prey, the sharks had learned to hit and hit hard. A full-on assault by a big white was often enough to bring the shark completely out of the water, tearing its target apart like a doll hit by a fang-bumpered truck.

Mason's life was saved by the smallest of unconscious actions – a split moment before the attack, he had stretched out into a swim, in effect, dodging the charging teeth at the very last instant.

Instead of hitting him dead center, the shark's jaws impacted on his leg, and the sheer violence of the attack was probably what saved Mason's life; the leg was severed and, while the impact knocked Colin's frail, two-hundred and thirty pound frame fifteen feet clear of the water, he had avoided the killing force of the blow. He had landed face-first and unconscious, floating head down, the water clouding redly with femoral blood.

Mason would almost certainly have died then if not for the security his father had always insisted he keep close at hand. Rather than organization types, Colin employed mostly mercs, ex-navy-seals and the like – trained in military combat medicine. Pulling him swiftly from the water, mindless of the circling shark, Mason's men managed to field-patch him enough for Life-flight to get him to a hospital.

The incident was immediately famous worldwide, even in the days before the Internet. Mason had taken a party out to the islands that day, and one of his guests had brought along a spendy new toy – a video camcorder. The entire incident – the attack, the shark rocketing from the water, Mason's life-flight rescue – was all captured on film, and the film sold promptly to the burgeoning cable news channels. In the weeks that followed, portions of the video received play several times a day.

Mason himself, disfigured and bed-ridden, had watched his tragedy on display for the gawking masses.

The third week following Colin's accident, the party guest who had filmed the attack disappeared from the party scene in California. Not a piece of him was ever found, but legend has it that the hapless opportunist found his own way back out to the

Farallons, and that his own encounter with its population of large sharks was filmed for posterity. It was further rumored that Mason kept the video record, along with others, in his own personal collection.

Colin Mason's convalescence lasted almost seven months, with physical therapy lasting for many months after. To those who knew him, Colin Mason after was much more fearsome than Colin Mason before, and like soured wine, only curdled over time.

And so, fourteen years passed.

CHAPTER 3

Mason's yacht was famously huge, with a massive, spacious main cabin with a bar and large screen cable TV, for which Mason paid a satellite connection by the hour – even he bitched about that bill when he got it. But it was all worth it, Mason said, because the Contest was his Christmas.

Alex hovered outside the door to the main cabin, surveying those inside. The guests or 'contestants' were easy to pick out of the dozen or so participants in the evening's revelry. One reason was that most of the rest were the token number of Mason's 'party girls,' all selected from the best massage parlors on the West Coast. Alex herself made it a point to stay clear of the early stages of the party, lest she be confused with one of Mason's party favors. She had been told by one contestant the previous year that the resemblance was there.

That particular contestant had been eliminated, Alex was happy to note.

There were four of them this year, and superficially, they all differed from those that came before. But in another way, Alex thought they all looked exactly the same. Their simply *being* there meant they all had a number of things in common with each other, and with all their predecessors. A cynical, third-year veteran of the Contest, Alex found herself struggling to see the differences between them.

Mason didn't pull his contestants out of a hat. There was actually a fairly strict selection process. The first and foremost was a need for money; Mason wished to establish control early on. Given the nature of the competition, Mason insisted on absolute assurance any… indiscretions… would remain confidential.

There were, however, a lot of people who needed money, who would go through a lot in order to get it; thus the next sorting category was that the contestant needed to be physically able to do it – physical fitness was a necessary requirement… for the contest itself was a race.

A swimming race, actually… through the Farallons. In shark season.

The prize: one million dollars.

And once seven figures entered the score sheet, there would never be a shortage of suicidal-minded hopefuls that would tap dance over the edge of a volcano for a million dollars; thus Mason imposed a third criteria that was at once the narrowest, yet most subjective of all: they had to be right for the Contest – this qualification was decided by Mason alone and overrode all others.

The loudest member of the party, and certainly the most jovial of this year's crop of contestants was case-in-point. He was a young guy, not much older than Alex herself, and could have passed for her brother with his sun-and-surf good-looks and California-blond hair. He called himself 'The Surfer Dude,' but he accepted checks in the name of Mick O'Brien.

In addition to being the youngest of this year's contestants, the Surfer Dude – 'Surf' to his friends, and to the number of party-girls presently dancing in his lap on the main couch – was a bit of departure in another, quite major way, that violated a border Alex had never seen Mason cross before.

It was a small thing, really, but the Surfer Dude had no particular debt or need of money. His was a life of waves and women and sleeping on the beach. He competed in surfing contests up and down the coast and had a following all along the California shore. He would have been happy to continue on that way forever. The simple fact was that in many ways he was just the sort of suicidal daredevil Mason ordinarily screened from his Contest: the Surfer Dude simply saw Mason's race as easy money; he genuinely had no fear of the sharks – which was remarkable since he'd been attacked twice himself.

A whoop rose up from Surfer Dude's small circle of friends. Surf was gesturing wildly at the TV screens, which, since night had fallen, had turned off the expensive cable-stations, and was now playing footage of the sharks in the Farallons, including many spectacular leaps and bloody kills. The shout from Surf and his five couch-mates was in response to a missed strike by a large shark at a seal - the twelve-foot torpedo-shaped body shot nearly fourteen-feet clear of the water.

Surfer Dude had first-hand experience in that kind of attack. And it was for this reason alone that Mason had given him his invitation: Surf's fame had preceded him.

Alex had first heard of the Surfer Dude four years before, when she'd moved down from Oregon. That had been his first attack and it had happened further south, down around Monterrey Point. Alex had been on the beach when the ambulance and TV crews had arrived. She'd seen Surfer Dude interviewed and walking, apparently unhurt, into the ambulance.

The shark had hit him from below, detonating like a bomb on the back half of his surfboard. The bite missed him cleanly but he was given a nasty scratch by a stiff, slapping fin. He had been close to shore and swam in himself. The ambulance was waiting for him when he got in. The shark had disappeared after the initial strike.

It was the second incident that had made him famous; like Mason's own attack, this one made it on camera, *and* occurred during the middle of the largest surfing competition of the summer. In almost the same exact spot as before, less than fourteen months later, Surfer Dude was hit again.

As before, the attack came from below, with the shark – a *big* shark by the bite on the surfboard – honing in on his surfboard like a little seal. Once again, the brunt of the attack missed him and he was flung bodily through the air. This time, however, he landed badly on the reefs, and then was washed out a moment later into the surf. Cut and bleeding in several places, he discovered that this time the shark hadn't disappeared but continued to circle interestedly as he made his way back to the beach. Footage from the National Sports TV video feed clearly showed the shark's tail fins slapping the water within fifteen feet of him, and the dorsal – with a moon-shaped crescent bitten out of it – veered constantly in his direction as he staggered out of the surf onto the beach.

Ironically, it was this incident that removed from his daredevil soul any last fear of sharks. "They aren't interested in us," he told the reporters that day. "He thought I was a seal. If he'd have wanted me, he was within ten feet of me all the way back to the beach. I was his."

By the end of the day, footage from his previous attack fourteen months before had been spliced in for a piece on Entertainment Tonight. Surfer Dude became a local celebrity, making cash for appearances at beach-related events. "Wine, women and song," he said to a camera at one point. "All for getting bit by a fish."

And as his entourage of lap dancers performed, the Surfer Dude jumped up on Mason's couch, shouting jubilantly over the speakers: "Hey! Mason! You gotta play mine! I know you got it!"

Mason, of course, was absent from the party this early on. Alex checked her watch – their host would be making his appearance soon enough.

The Surfer Dude collapsed back onto the couch, into his circle of well-paid beauties. He stared, happily drunk and starry-eyed, at all of them together. "I'm famous, you know," he told them. "And I'm gonna win this race tomorrow."

Alex found herself smiling. Surfer Dude was the only one of the contestants who was really putting it away – like Alex herself, he was young and invulnerable. And his confidence only increased with the high octanes.

"I'm the fastest swimmer, I'll bet," he boasted, enjoying the truth of it, which was at least the truth through a skinful of Jack Daniel's. "All I have to do is not get bit by anything and the money's mine," he said, smiling broadly.

On the big screen TV, another seal was blasted skyward as another big shark rocketed out of the surf from below. Sitting quietly in an easy chair behind the couch party, one of the other contestants, this one a smallish, dark-haired and bearded man, leaned forward and asked, "What makes you think you won't get bit?"

The Surfer Dude frowned, turned and regarded the speaker. He shrugged. "It's like I tell people – they don't like the taste of us. If white sharks wanted to eat people, they'd eat a lot more of them. 'Cause there's a lot of sharks out there."

"That's true," the bearded man said. "But in such a high-volume prey-environment, it might not matter."

Surfer Dude's frown deepened. The bearded man smiled. "Look at those screens," he said, indicating the TV screen and yet another demolished elephant seal with another shark flying acrobatically clear of the water. "Those are full-on attacks." The bearded man's smile widened. "The sharks in the Farallons hit… and they hit hard."

Surfer Dude looked up at the screen uncertainly. Then he shrugged. "Ahh, they still don't want *us*." Dismissing the topic, he turned back to his couch party. The bearded man shook his head, then turned and caught Alex smiling at him. His face brightened.

Alex turned away quickly; she didn't want that kind of attention – she had only been smiling at Surfer Dude's reaction. Alex stared steadfastly in the other direction but it didn't help; the bearded man rose and walked over anyway, sitting down on the couch and gesturing at the screen.

"Those are my movies," he told her.

Alex, of course, had known that already; her association with Mason had actually brought her to feel she knew this man quite well, even though this was the first time she'd actually seen him in person. He was this year's oldest contestant and Alex knew Mason considered his presence a bit of a coup. He was none other than Dr. Stephen Dreyfuss – the very same who had filmed much of the shark footage on screen right now.

"There I am," Dreyfuss said, smiling broadly, pointing at a much younger version of himself prodding a camera on a stick into the maw of an eighteen-foot white shark as it fed lazily on a seal's carcass.

Alex smiled indulgently, reading the level of alcohol in Dreyfuss' eyes. He was probably trying to take it easy, she decided, but he had already passed the point of relaxed inhibitions. She hoped he would give up before Mason came down – Mason would get pissy about it. Not to Dreyfuss, of course, not his honored contestants... but he might be a real pain in the ass – literally – for her later that night.

Dreyfuss was making an attempt at small talk, which Alex parried easily without really paying attention. She studied Dreyfuss' face and reviewed some of the things she knew about him. As Mason's companion, she'd known about the good doctor long before he ever became a contestant; Dreyfuss had produced the best shark footage anywhere in the world. She knew about his life, marriage and his divorce.

And of course, she also knew that he needed money.

"I got divorced recently," Dreyfuss was telling Alex, telling her nothing she didn't already know. Mason researched his contestants like players on his favorite football team, and in the months before his annual event, he often talked of little else. Alex knew about Dreyfuss' divorce, along with the rest of the unfortunate circumstances that had brought him, like others before him, on board.

Stephen Dreyfuss' professional life had been tumultuous from the start, ironically nothing like the situation that broke up his marriage. Dreyfuss in his professional life was driven, ambitious, willing to take crazy – some would say suicidal – risks just to get a better shot on film.

His home life was quite the opposite. His wife, Janet Marsh-Dreyfuss, was quiet and demure - at heart they were both academics, which was how they met at UCLA. While Stephen was a science-guy, Janet's degree was in literature and they provided a nice comfortable balance for each other. Stephen's professional troubles, however, had cascaded like an unexpected tidal wave onto the quiet comfort of their relationship; Janet had never been the sort who wanted to be on Time magazine, and eventually she had to leave.

Dreyfuss' work problems were, in a roundabout way, a result of the very thing that made him famous - his videos. While exciting to the public and great for the academics – that is to say 'non-field agents' – because it generated fund money, it also branded Stephen a bit of a Maverick – heavily frowned on in academic circles ruled by orthodoxy. In addition, his footage was not simply show business; it documented conclusively aspects about shark behavior that had only been theorized before. Unfortunately, many of those theories that Stephen's footage blasted out of the water had been first proposed by individuals still living and occupying important positions in the doctorate community. And in the manner of the deeply learned, when presented with new and exciting ideas they did their best to squelch them like annoying and dangerous bugs and swept the crumbs under the carpet.

The academic troubles Stephen would have eventually worked through; he was amiable and willing to pay enough dues to *earn* his respect before his superiors. It was his documentaries that brought him his real trouble – and from an entirely unexpected direction.

Dreyfuss actually saw his own subpoena on television before he was even served. He returned late one night to see some kind of legal-envelope taped to his door, which he tossed aside for the moment, ignoring also the beeping of messages on his answering machine. Janet had been away at her mother's.

He turned on the news to see himself, standing up in a boat, his camera extended towards the jaws of a large shark feeding hungrily on a whale carcass – it had been a juvenile humpback, Stephen remembered. It had probably died sick.

Stephen listened to himself narrate along as he filmed, turning the camera towards the surrounding ocean. "Only the largest shark feeds first," his TV-self said. "It's a pecking order. There are usually several sharks circling below that we don't see."

It was from his first video, and the moment was a favorite as the camera had caught his assistant, a doubtful-looking college student who didn't know he was going to be driving this little fucking boat out to where giant sharks were eating seals: "You can't possibly be paying me enough for this shit, man."

"Keep the boat steady," had been Dreyfuss' videotaped response. "This is a big shark."

The camera on a stick technique had been great for close-ups, but it couldn't hold a candle to the dramatic surfboard shots, with the board and its reinforced camera floated out past the rocks. First, there would be nothing but depthless blue ocean, facing straight down into the deep. Then out of the gloom the shark would come rocketing, jaws agape, tail pumping with all the explosive power of its two-ton body. The teeth would hit the board like a locomotive, sometimes shattering the lens. But the film survived and made him famous.

Some of the stars of Stephen's films also became famous. Part of their research had consisted of tagging and cataloging different sharks off the Pacific Coast. They found that the same sharks usually appeared at the Farallons year after year. One in particular they had numerous records of; she was one of the largest and most aggressive; an eighteen-plus foot female they had nicknamed 'Sandy,' whom they had recorded in no less than a dozen attacks on seals and on their decoy boards.

Sandy turned up dutifully every two years – apparently, part of a global migration – and was recognizable by the moon-shaped crescent bitten out of her dorsal fin. Named as she was after the only white shark ever to be successfully kept in, and subsequently released from captivity, Sandy became a quasi-fictional celebrity not unlike 'Nessie.' Dreyfuss, as career-minded as any professional researcher, used the opportunity to point out that the same sharks were attacking his decoys year after year, which legitimized many of his own ideas concerning shark behavior, particularly those concerning migration and social behavior.

It was, however, a different kind of shark behavior that caused most of Dreyfuss' troubles.

It was not the double attack by a big white off the coast of San Francisco's that Stephen didn't see coming. He understood that. Two surfers, a young newly-wed husband and bride had been hit in the surf by a very large shark, unquestionably a white – possibly Sandy herself – and both man and wife had been killed. The young woman, Tracy Morgan, whose maiden name had been Vandenhausen, had washed ashore two days later... or at least her mid torso had. The semi-circular wounds were clearly from the jaws of a Great White.

Stephen had heard about the attack several days before, of course, and regarded it as a tragedy – but he was stunned a moment later when the same story came on directly following his own video cameo. The newscaster then served Stephen with the summons Tracy Vandenhausen-Morgan's father's lawyer had been knocking on his door for all day.

The legal-looking envelope was a copy of the summons. Apparently, the senior Vandenhausen had become convinced – probably by his lawyers – that Dreyfuss' own videos provided incontrovertible proof that Stephen had been teaching sharks to attack surfboards.

Dreyfuss had laughed out loud when he first read the document. He stopped laughing the next day when his own lawyer informed him that the Vandenhausen family commanded considerable wealth, and were at the moment contributing large sums of it to the cause of putting Stephen Dreyfuss in jail for the rest of his life. A civil suit would take his meager belongings as a trifle.

Stephen didn't really start getting scared until he saw the Vandenhausen's highly-paid squad of legal hit men on TV. If their moralities were bought, they gave their clients full-value. By the time they were done with that first press conference, Dreyfuss felt like he knew both victims personally and was almost compelled to turn himself in as an accessory.

His academic superiors were also less than supportive.

The simple, scientific fact, however, was that Stephen's culpability was patently non-existent; he wasn't 'teaching' the sharks to attack the boards – they did that anyway. He was simply triggering a natural impulse that had already existed for a hundred million years… the same impulse triggered by the surfboards of the Vandenhausen's unfortunate daughter and her husband.

Such facts, however, couldn't hold a candle to the drama painted by the Vandenhausen lawyers, and sure enough, the case went to court. With Stephen Dreyfuss' life and fortune on the line, the jury had actually ruled *against* him. Completely swayed by the legal theatrics and opportunistic morality of the Vandenhausen legal team, they had gone against Stephen with their full weight - maximum sentence, Manslaughter, Wrongful Death, the whole bit. The judge in the case, however, had come to Stephen's rescue; he employed a little-used prerogative and overturned the jury's decision – the scientific evidence was incontrovertible as far as the judge was concerned, never mind the doubtful link to Stephen Dreyfuss and the actual attacking shark – Sandy or no Sandy.

Ironically, most of Stephen's legal problems were with his own lawyer, who, after actually *losing* his case, was still happy enough to collect his fee, and spent the next fourteen months breaking Stephen's bank accounts down to nothing.

Professionally as well, Stephen's life was in a nosedive. Others had begun to mimic his camera techniques; by now, it had all been seen and duplicated, requiring that he come up with ever more innovative and daring experiments for each succeeding project. And the videos had become his sole income. The academic world had abandoned him like rats deserting a sinking ship. His funding, as a result, was halved, as was the budget for his video projects.

And somewhere in the middle, he had lost his wife.

The initial court case was probably a mortal blow to the marriage all on its own; the first time Janet had walked out on her nice, quiet porch, with the expectation of nothing more than retrieving her morning paper and perhaps sipping her morning coffee, and was confronted by the onslaught of a mob of cameras and reporters, the quiet security of their relationship was shattered. They hung on, their relationship sick and dying, for the next several months, through the trial, the mounting bills, and the media, holding on together almost until the end.

Then she had gone.

At work, Stephen Dreyfuss had changed. People on his own crews began to doubt him. The joyful, if obsessive interest had been replaced by an angry, punishing recklessness that even his most loyal friends couldn't ignore.

There was, for instance, the time he'd weighted his rusting old shark cage to the ocean floor, and stepped out, free-swimming with three, very large circling whites, poking them with a long stick whenever they drew too close. His own cameraman, filming from another cage, had nearly hyperventilated in his air-mask, waiting as Stephen baited the sharks ever closer before finally retreating into his cage.

Then there was the time he'd climbed out on top of a sperm whale carcass that had drifted into the Farallons. The sharks had frenzied around the fifty-foot, floating island, and Stephen had taken his camcorder out onto the whale's ice-slick hide, actually pushing the lens down into the feeding jaws of the dozen or so big whites that hurled themselves out of the water, tearing away great chunks of blubber, sending vibrations all the way back up to the boat. On Stephen's own film, his crew could be heard shouting, with nominal anger but tainted with mounting hysteria, exhorting him, begging him to come back. Once, he nearly slipped, which would have dropped him right in among the chomping, smashing jaws.

Eventually, as his stunts grew ever more reckless, his old crew abandoned him one by one. And as his reputation had now become dubious, it became difficult just getting people to rent him a boat, let alone come along. His work, his last refuge, was in danger of being taken from him.

In the end, it was just him and his camera. His career was over, and even the seedier distributors were unwilling to see him continue. His contracts were canceled, his marriage was over, and he still owed more money than he could ever make. At thirty-three, Stephen Dreyfuss was finished.

And like a lion separating a zebra from a herd, Colin Mason had stepped in and made Dreyfuss his offer. Having no other particular reason to live, and given the possibility of a new start, Stephen had said yes.

And as Alex listened to Stephen tell his by-now, well-known story, she recognized all the signs of the beaten-down, but still hopeful. She particularly recognized the randiness of a freshly divorced man – she'd been the other woman enough times to know. She was, however, spared the effort of having to turn him down by the interruption of the third member of that year's group of contestants.

If Stephen Dreyfuss had made the local papers, Kurt Wagner had been on the cover of Sports Illustrated; he would have made it to a Wheaties box later that same year if his life – like most of Mason's contestants – hadn't suddenly up and turned to shit.

Wagner was an Olympic swimmer; tall, lanky and muscular, with a handsome, troubled face, much different from the Surfer Dude's casual good-looks. Alex herself had scoped him out thoroughly when he'd come on board the morning before. Like Dreyfuss, he had caught her glance, but had ignored her at the time, just as he had the rest of Mason's troop of party-girls.

Now however, he abruptly abandoned the lounging chair he'd commandeered in the corner all night, saying nothing, watching Mason's videos with no more than casual interest; he rose and walked over to where Alex was fending off Dreyfuss and sat down.

Dreyfuss' face registered obvious displeasure but Wagner ignored him, speaking directly to Alex herself.

"What's your function here?" he asked.

"What do you mean?" Alex said. "I'm a guest, just like you."

Wagner shook his head. "No one here is a guest. Are you one of Mason's bimbos-for-hire?"

Dreyfuss blanched but Alex was ignoring him now too. She stared back at Kurt Wagner, recalling the details Mason had told her about him. She remembered that some of his more publicized troubles had come as a result of his own mouth.

Alex supposed she could respect that. Her own mouth remained on a constant leash. She stared back at Wagner, unintimidated.

"I'm just a friend," she said. "I'm just a friend who's here because Mason wants me here."

"You mean you're Mason's *personal* bimbo," Kurt said.

Dreyfuss cleared his voice. "Listen, that's kind of rude..."

Alex wasn't listening. Wagner was staring at her in an intense, curious way – almost angrily. It was Alex' experience that athletes – the intelligent ones – were often angry. And Kurt Wagner had been America's Golden Boy for a brief stretch. He had just won four Olympic Gold Medals in four events. Tall, handsome and media-friendly, with a heroic air of confidence, he was made for a public that was desperate for heroes.

This made the backlash worse when, just a few short weeks after the Olympics, it was revealed he had tested positive for steroids. All four medals were summarily stripped. Kurt Wagner's decline, however, had already started before that; the drug test had registered a pain-killing medication he had unknowingly taken for a pulled tendon – it was a legitimate misunderstanding that Kurt might have weathered through if his publicity hadn't already taken a marked turn for the worse in preceding weeks.

When the cloud of misfortune had settled in on Kurt Wagner's life, it was the equal and opposite reaction that countered the glory of his Olympic victories. One week after the medals had been placed around his head, Kurt's wife, Anna, who had been a popular Olympic alternate, was diagnosed with cancer; and just that quickly, two weeks later, she died.

Kurt had died that day too, in any way that counted. He had been coming home from his wife's funeral when the steroid-story first broke. The two items were profiled together on the news. And when the flood of reporters invaded his home in the following days, Kurt sounded off at them in anger and grief. In the days following, a lot of alcohol was thrown into the mixture as well.

He might have recovered from Anna's passing if he'd simply been allowed. But the storm cloud followed him along. Immediately after his Olympic disgrace, a reporter named Greeley, a sharp-faced, weaselly, condescending little shit, had thrust a microphone in his face and asked, "Are you at least glad Anna didn't live to see this?"

Kurt had turned, slowly, recognizing Greeley from his own front porch the day his wife had died. "I would do anything," Kurt said, "*anything*, if I could have her back again."

Then he had slugged Greeley dead in the face.

The little bastard was still unconscious when the ambulance arrived. The other members of the press, as protective of their own as a swarm of wasps, turned on him in shock and anger. The steroid issue was heavily publicized and when it was revealed that Kurt's drug infraction had been unintentional, it made page three with a small-face headline. In addition, Greeley, who had stretched his stay in the hospital to almost ten days, was preparing both criminal and civil charges.

Once the trouble started it began to landslide. In the months following, there were a number of other incidents. Two of them were drug-related; the second had been a double bill – a coke-bust with some starlet who, unbeknownst to Kurt, was a former prostitute who routinely carried around half a gram of powder for daily use.

This and other incidents led to the loss of promising endorsement deals, not to mention a possible acting career. And to add insult to injury, he was no longer allowed to compete in legitimate swimming events.

And Mason had been there waiting when Kurt Wagner had hit rock bottom.

He was this year's favorite.

Alex met Kurt's challenging, steely eyes directly, never letting on that he was indeed pissing her off, just like he wanted to. Kurt, however, wasn't done.

"What's it like having a free ride?" Kurt asked her.

Alex smiled. "You know, you're not so pure," she said. "You're here for his money too."

Kurt glanced up at the large video screen as yet another elephant seal disappeared into the protruding jaws of a large

Carcharodon. He gestured around them, indicating the ocean outside, the same ocean in which that very scene had been filmed.

"Yeah," Kurt said, "but my ride's not free."

Alex settled down into the couch. Meeting Kurt's eyes directly, she drew back the sash on her robe. The smooth tan skin of her legs glistened in the dim lights of the cabin. She rubbed her legs together like a grasshopper and then spread her legs, revealing the thong-stringed bikini. When she spoke, her voice was a hiss.

"My ride's not free either," she said.

Kurt eyed her back. "Fair enough," he said, and with that, he stood, nodded for the first time at Dreyfuss, who was still sitting there open-mouthed, and stepped quietly away. Alex turned her gaze over to Stephen.

"You heard him, honey," Alex said. "I'm spoken for."

Stephen's shoulders slumped; he stood and walked morosely over to the bar. Kurt ambled up next to him and sat down and, despite his confidential tone, Alex could hear perfectly as Kurt told Stephen, "Don't let it get you down. Women like that have teeth in their pussies anyway."

Kurt tossed a glance over his shoulder, making sure Alex had heard. Alex acted as if she had not.

The Surfer Dude's entourage had grown and Kurt slapped Stephen on the back. "Why don't you go after one of those bleach-blondes," he suggested. "That's what they're here for."

Alex grinned despite herself. She could see Dreyfuss' pride wouldn't let him go there yet. And that left only one available woman on board – his eyes turned to Amber Thiessen, who was the fourth and final contestant in this year's Contest, and the first female racer in all Alex's years with Mason.

Besides her gender, Amber was unique among almost all other contestants because Alex knew almost nothing about her. Mason had not even mentioned a fourth contestant until the day before the event. He also hadn't mentioned she was a woman.

Alex studied Amber with a critical eye. She was pretty in a brooding sort of way – like if Kurt Wagner had a sister. Amber's midsection was exposed in an athletic stretch top and her abdomen was taut with muscle. Her legs as well were long and muscular like a dancer's.

Stephen Dreyfuss had also noticed Amber's legs and Alex was amused to see him gather himself, moseying up to her like a clumsy pass in a singles bar. Alex shook her head, trying to reconcile this stuttering idiot with the dramatic films he'd made – close ups in most cases – of giant sharks, snapping and fighting over whale carcasses. Amber barely spared Stephen a sideways glance, simply standing without saying a word, dismissing him like a mare swatting at a fly with her tail. Dreyfuss sat there stunned, his eyes turning with reluctant interest to Mason's party girls.

Alex's eyes followed Amber as she crossed the room, watching how she kept her eyes consciously away from the TV screens and Mason's shark videos. She found a small cushioned love seat in the corner and sat down. Then she looked up and saw Alex watching her.

For a moment Alex, who rarely, if ever, felt a threat from a woman, was taken aback. The smoking gleam that came into Amber's eyes was like an agitated rattlesnake. The intimidation was so primal Alex reacted instinctively, breaking eye-contact and looking away. Surprised and ashamed at her own weakness, she forced herself to look back. Amber was still staring venomously, but Alex had the guard up over her eyes now, and she was safe.

She wondered, however, as Amber finally looked away disinterestedly, what her connection was with Mason – there had to be something; the woman's intensity, combined with her mysterious entry in the contest, made Alex nervous.

It meant that Mason was playing games – and one that Alex noted didn't include her.

Amber's story, however, would have to wait, for Mason himself chose that very moment to make his first appearance of the evening.

Mason, who always spent the early part of the evening before race day apart from the festivities, had been sequestered all night in the Captain's cabin that adjoined to the bridge. Often he would retire up there with several members of his current party girl troop; Alex couldn't have cared less – she could use the break. Most of the massage parlor girls were vacuous and spacey, distant in conversation, without the necessary depth to move in on Mason in any serious way. Alex judged them as no threat whatsoever.

Her eyes cut back over to Amber, who was now pointedly looking in the other direction.

That was when the TV's video-feed suddenly cut off and Mason's music – Mac the Knife – came on the speakers. Mason liked to make an entrance; liked hearing his name bantered about and watching heads in the cabin turn as he appeared at the door with his entourage of party girls.

Like the shark videos, it was Mason's way of bringing his gleeful game of psychological warfare to the next stage…

CHAPTER 4

Colin Mason, despite increased weight and advancing years, not to mention his right leg missing from just below the hip, remained a powerful and intimidating presence. He liked to make his appearance with the smallest touch of drama, appearing for the first time of the night with his closest personal bodyguard, Roland Mercer, standing behind his wheelchair bearing an uncomfortable similarity to the Terminator. 'Mac the Knife's' pretty shark teeth played over the speakers. Mason enjoyed the small silence from his audience in the cabin.

Mercer, the bodyguard, cut quite a sight all by himself. He was a big guy, with hard, steel gray eyes that were perpetually hidden by blankly mirrored sunglasses, which had always reminded Alex of Mason's sharks. That was probably why Mason trusted him, she thought; Mercer was a *human* predator.

Mason himself, settled comfortably with his one leg in his stylized wheelchair, was like a fat, old, but battle-scarred tomcat, one living richly and luxuriously, but retaining lethal claws. His sheath of party-fat concealed muscle that remained hard through regular exercise – he still swam like a fish – and his eyes were every bit as carnivorous as his mercenary bodyguard. Together the two of them created a chilling portrait that was not softened in the least by Mason's own Carcharodon-like smile.

The room was appropriately subdued and the shark smile widened. Mason caught Alex's eyes across the room and she could see he was enjoying the effect. He waited for just the right moment to break the spell.

"Good evening, everyone!" Mason said finally, addressing the room as one. 'Mac the Knife' faded. "Is everybody having a good time?"

Surfer Dude recovered first, his youthful confidence flowing back. He whistled out, squeezing the buns of two of his party-favors, causing them to squeal out as well. "It's a party, dude!" he hollered back. "Come on, Mason, you gotta play my video!" Surfer Dude's entourage giggled affirmative.

Mason's smile relaxed into a grin. Behind him, the stone-faced Mercer produced a videocassette from the back of Mason's chair.

"As it happens, Mr. O'Brien," Mason said, addressing Surfer Dude by his check-signing name, "video is exactly what I have to show you." For a moment, the Carcharodon crept back into Mason's smile. "However, this particular show is a touch more graphic than your thoroughly televised incident." Mason nodded to Stephen. "You especially might enjoy this, Mr. Dreyfuss," he said. "Like the bulk of your own work, this footage was all shot right here in the Farallons. My camera techniques are, of course, not as innovative as your own, but I hope you will take imitation as flattery."

Mercer snapped Mason's video into the player at the back of the room and darkened the lights. Over in her corner, Alex grimaced to herself; she hated this part.

"You all understand," Mason's voice said in the darkened room, "that I must have your complete discretion concerning these videos." His voice was dry and easy, and very matter of fact. "They are highly illegal – in fact, in California they would be considered 'Snuff' films." The voice grew friendly and wise like a respected Grandfather as he assured everyone that; "If anyone ever breathes a word of these tapes to anyone after the contest, Mr. Mercer will be pitching you overboard here in these very islands."

Mason chuckled in the darkness as the video flickered and began. Alex heard not a stutter from anyone; the anticipation was palpable and for the first time tonight the contestants were being directly confronted with what they had come here to do.

They all knew about Mason's race-tapes of course; they were part of the legend. They also knew Mason would make them watch. Because Mason filmed everything. Emulating Stephen Dreyfuss' own techniques, Mason followed each swimmer with men in boats. The boats were ostensibly there to provide a modicum of safety for the swimmer; they shared a dual purpose, however, allowing Mason's camera to be right there handy whenever a contestant was... well, eliminated.

It was the only competition tape in the world where the highlights were from all the losers.

As the video began, unobtrusively showing a number of unremarkable-looking swimmers, diving off the back of Mason's yacht, Alex recognized a number of faces from the previous year's Contest, from this same party one year before. She glanced down at this year's batch as they leaned attentively forward. Dreyfuss and Surfer Dude were up on their haunches, and Amber seemed to be staring riveted, face half-turned but unable to look away. Only

Kurt sat back relaxed, but even his eyes remained locked on the screen and his brooding face had gone set and grim.

On screen, the swimmers were being profiled one by one, cutting back and forth to close-ups of the competitors in the water with footage from the party. Mason's own voice provided the narrative, clearly mimicking Dreyfuss' documentary style. Personality sketches were quick but detailed; Mason felt that it was important that his current guests recognized the reality of the people they were watching.

Of course, over fourteen years there had been a lot of Contests. There was a lot of footage to choose from, providing a couple of other visual zingers for Mason to throw at his guests.

Stephen Dreyfuss, for example, leaned forward startled, as Mason's video voice introduced a bearded contestant that could have passed for his brother. Another character profile showed a guy that looked a lot like Kurt, apparently in the same race.

It was the Kurt look-alike that was eliminated first.

In slow motion it looked just like one of Dreyfuss' videos, with the shark suddenly bursting from the ocean like a liquid rocket – but this time the tattered shape falling in pieces from either side of the jaw was no seal.

A human is gangly and frail compared to a seal. A solid hit by a big white was proven by Mason's video to be quite sufficient to blast a full-grown man into flying pieces. The subsequent feeding took less than a minute, with the shark returning to casually chomp up the refuse.

The shark's dorsal passed within clear view of the camera. The crescent-shaped scar was visible.

"That's Sandy," Stephen said, clearing his voice uncomfortably. "Jesus."

"Yes," Mason said from behind him. "I wondered if you'd recognize her. You will see several sharks I'm sure you've documented personally. Sandy is a bit of a star of my own series as well."

The Dreyfuss look-alike went a moment later. Same as before, the attack came from below, cutting its bearded target cleanly in half. Dreyfuss noted that the camera was close; if filmed from a boat that meant the swimmer had probably been making a run for it – he had known the shark was in the area. This time the shark's dorsal fin remained below the surface, but the attacker was at least a full-grown female, in the eighteen-foot range. The close-up camera clearly showed the bearded man's face, still connected to the shoulder, floating for nearly a minute before the cavernous mouth appeared from below and snapped it up like a giant goldfish.

The documentary cut to another race, this one featuring a tall, blond surfer-type, who was laughing and joking at the party the night before the race, projecting his personality right through the camera. Alex wondered at the depth of Mason's video archives – he had clearly weeded this compilation out of an extensive file.

This year's own Surfer Dude was leaning forward avidly. "Oh, man, that's me. That ain't even funny, man."

The film cut to the ocean and Surfer Dude's counterpart reaching frantically for the boat, one of Mason's guards, perhaps Mercer himself, reaching for the swimmer's flailing arm. The cameraman, however, never wavered, focusing on the victim's wide, pleading eyes and reaching hands as the attack came from below.

Others. A tall redheaded basketball player, a small Hawaiian diver, another athlete like Kurt, all hit from below. It began to take on a certain brutal redundancy. "Jesus," Surfer Dude finally blurted out, "Does anyone ever win this, Mason?"

Mason's smile was visible in the dark, once again mimicking an old tomcat, perhaps a Cheshire version. "I assure you," Mason said, "we have had a winner every single year; not once have we ever lost every single swimmer." Then came the low chuckle. "Of course, we do lose *somebody*. Every time. Every year."

On screen the carnage continued – way more carnage, Alex reflected, than would be justified from even fourteen years of Contests. Some of this footage had to have been filmed in the 'off-season.' Such details, however, might slip past a first-time viewer.

And Mason's assurance of a yearly winner was never actually confirmed by video; every person profiled so far had already been eaten. No doubt, the contestants here tonight were remembering their own videotaped interviews, perhaps wondering who might be a part of next year's highlight reel.

Abruptly, the videos stopped and the cabin lights came on. This was also a calculated move, Alex knew – Mason wanted to give the impression that the attack archives were endless and that only time constraints caused him to interrupt.

But before the videos clicked off, one final scene – Stephen Dreyfuss himself, holding the bitten surfboard, glancing over his shoulder at the rough water of the Farallons.

"Don't get me wrong," Dreyfuss said onscreen, "I wouldn't go swimming out *here* for anything."

Then the video feed quit and the screen went black.

There was dead silence in the room.

Mason's psychological game was clearly working on Dreyfuss, who sat frowning, staring at the screen after his own face. Of the group, Alex knew that, despite his close association with both sharks and the ocean, Stephen had no particular competitive athletic experience, and some of the simple tricks seemed to be working on him. Kurt Wagner sat through the show as if bored – and the Surfer Dude actually seemed to enjoy it. Alex figured their reactions were probably affected at least to a degree, although the Surfer Dude did seem to live on the particular adrenaline associated with fear. Stephen, however, was wringing his hands as the lights came on.

Amber too, Alex saw, looked pale and scared as Mason tapped his glass, commanding attention once again.

"Stage One begins tomorrow at dawn," Mason said, his voice all business now. "I suggest you all get some rest."

Surfer Dude raised his hand.

"Hey Mason," he said, "After I win, how soon do I get paid?"

Mason never smiled where money was concerned. "The winner will be paid immediately when the race is over." He cast a stern eye upon Surfer Dude and then on the rest. "Sleep well, my friends. The lights will go off in one hour."

Mercer steered Mason past Alex towards the door. "Will you be needing me tonight?" she asked.

Mason smiled, gesturing to two of his fresh-faced party girls – both as vacuous and blank as if they hadn't just sat through the Animal Planet's version of a Snuff film. Mason tipped his hat to Alex. "Take the night off," he told her.

The lights began to steadily dim. Surfer Dude took the hint, retiring to his room with his five well-paid beauties. Stephen Dreyfuss cast one last hopeful eye at Amber – who responded with a sniff and rolled eyelids – and then at Alex herself, before walking with a shrug over to the remaining crowd of Mason's call girls. He selected one that looked exactly like Pamela Anderson Lee and took Surfer Dude's lead, disappearing with his pre-paid-date into his own room.

Kurt Wagner remained a while longer, ignoring Mason's bimbos, his eyes settling with their bored, brooding expression on Alex's own. She wondered if he had heard Mason giving her the night off; she wondered if she'd let him if he hit on her.

But instead, Kurt stood, ignoring both Alex and Mason's party-girls as he retired to his own room alone.

That left Amber and Alex sitting there alone. The rest of Mason's party troop would be taken ashore by some of Mercer's men, and most of them were already gathering their things. Alex kept her eye on Amber, still a touch shamed at being stared down earlier – it had been a rare experience in her short-but-eventful life. Amber, however, ignored her, sitting in the dimming light, staring out at the ocean. When she finally rose from her chair, she passed Alex with a bare sidelong glance and a sniff of dismissal.

Alex sipped her wine, reflecting that if Amber were to be eliminated tomorrow, she would have Mason make an extra copy of the video for her own collection.

The lights on the yacht were set on a timer that now faded out. Alex sat there in the dark, listening to the motors heat up as Mercer's men escorted the dateless ladies of the evening back to shore. When they had gone, Alex rose and made her way back up on deck, stretching out in her sun-warmed lawn chair, where she would spend the night.

It was warm under the stars, and the moon was past three-quarters full. On the distant horizon, the sky was still pink and the flat surface of the ocean was broken by the jagged rocks of the Farallons.

And beneath that mirrored surface, Alex knew the sharks waited.

CHAPTER 5

Dawn in the Farallons was every bit as beautiful as the sunset, with the needling rays of the sun creeping past the distant California land mass, lighting the ocean like diamond chain mail; it is doubtful, however, if any of Colin Mason's current crop of racers were in a frame of mind to be truly appreciative of the ocean's idyllic beauty. Perhaps the Surfer Dude, who bugled a few bars of the National Anthem as he stood on the night-cooled deck, and who lived on adrenaline. Nevertheless, they'd all had moments of uneasy sleep during the night – flitting bits of dreams inter-spliced with the reality of Mason's videos.

The sea was flat as gelatin and, as the four of them stood shivering in the breeze of the ocean morning, knowing the temperature would soon skyrocket, Stephen Dreyfuss heard his own voice, remarking in his first video, that luring a shark was a lot like trout fishing.

Today, he thought unhappily, would be a great day for trout fishing.

The race would begin from the deck of Mason's yacht, and the first day's swim would take them nearly ten miles to the first island. The ocean, despite the sun's heat, would remain cold; the summer weather was irrelevant to the sea.

In the water, awaiting the start of the race were Mason's four 'guard-boats,' one for each swimmer. The boats were each manned by two of Mason's mercenary bodyguards, under the command of

Mercer, and who could have all passed for his brothers – or possibly his robotic clones. Each man carried weapons, but one on each boat also carried a camera... recording this year's highlights.

The Trailer-boats' stated purpose, of course, was more benign; besides a camera, each boat was also provided a small, slender, seemingly irrelevant-looking tube.

Stephen Dreyfuss, however, recognized the item as the very latest in shark-repellent technology; his own idea, in fact, which he had tossed off blithely to the public in one of his own videos, never thinking about the possibility of marketing the item himself. Stephen actually felt a bit of relief at seeing the device in the boat-men's hands, for although it was a method of shark-deterrent that had never been widely used before, all preliminary tests had met with unqualified success.

It so happens that sharks, and particularly white sharks, are hypersensitive to electricity. Sandy, the juvenile female that had been held captive for two weeks and who was also the namesake for the Farallons' Sandy, showed a marked sensitivity and debilitation from the low watt electricity that powered the lights and pumps in her aquarium. It was Sandy's severe reaction to the tiny voltage that prompted her keepers to release her into the wild before she died.

Stephen Dreyfuss was the one who connected the dots, theorizing that electricity might work as an effective deterrent. It had been a tossed off the shoulder comment near the end of his second video – Stephen was usually more interested in *attracting* sharks – but he heard a few months down the line that other scientists had been experimenting with the idea.

It was Colin Mason himself that ran with the idea; Dreyfuss had heard he was nearly ready with a commercial model of the device his men carried on the boats. Mason's own version of the 'Shark-Zapper' was, of course, quite a bit more high-budget than the nickel and dime palm-buzzers some of Dreyfuss' research-grant colleagues had experimented with. From what Stephen had heard, the only reason the product line hadn't already gone commercial were safety concerns about an electrical device with a powerful current designed for use in water.

Mason's publicly-printed response to that was "Better electrocuted than bitten in half."

Still, Mason's ideas all looked promising; the electric charge was not intended to be lethal and there were several different spins on the basic idea. One was intended as a survival item for shipwrecked sailors, lost at sea, floating in groups just like in the old World War Two days, left at the mercy of packs of oceanic white-tip sharks, every bit as voracious and aggressive as the highly dangerous bull shark. Horror stories of feeding-frenzied massacres provided the inspirations for Mason's 'Pulse-buzzer,' which released a generalized pulse of electricity every five to ten minutes, scattering any gathered sharks like a finger tapping the glass on a goldfish bowl.

The basic device, however, the one that Mason's men carried on the boats, was a no-nonsense, and yet non-lethal weapon – perfect, as it drew no blood. The 'Shark-Zapper' or 'Shark-Stick' – they were still toying with the name – essentially mirrored the appearance of the traditional 'powerhead,' an old fashioned underwater gun that fired a single shotgun shell. The Shark-Stick was a dramatic improvement in a number of ways, not the least of which in that it could be fired from a distance rather than pressed against the shark's head, and that it could be fired repeatedly. In all tests so far, sharks had retreated immediately from the vicinity of an activated device.

It could not, however, physically *stop* the attack of a charging white – like a gun it was only effective on the attack you saw coming, and then only if it was out and ready.

Besides, Mason liked to make his swimmers earn their money.

The Shark-Stick was a courtesy, and one whose purpose was clearly defined in the rules; one of the final requirements was that each swimmer be thoroughly familiar with the Contest rules, often imposing a written test in the days before the race – he wanted everyone very clear on the stakes.

Not, Mason replied when Kurt Wagner asked, that he'd ever actually turned down anyone at this late stage of the game for flunking his quiz.

The primary rule Mason wanted his swimmers to understand was his concept of 'Outs'; an Out was an option a swimmer could employ in the event of an imminent attack – he could be pulled by Mercer's men into the safety of their trailer boat. This was where the shark-stick came in. Each racer was allowed three Outs an hour, before being penalized. A penalty was a deduction of distance wherein the trailer boat simply turned and headed with the swimmer back in the direction it had come, for the fifteen-minute time-limit afforded for an Out. If the boat reaches its start or the racer accumulates three penalties then that swimmer is disqualified.

The race was in three stages, over the course of three days. The first night, tonight, they would camp out on the first of the islands, the largest of the chain and the one on which the coast guard had mounted the lighthouse. They would probably be bunking in close association with a number of seals; even in the morning stillness, and the stretch of miles between the first of the islands, the honking of elephant seals could be heard, echoing in the distance like the calls of gulls.

Big fat elephant seals – the white shark's favorite prey.

Stephen Dreyfuss cast another baleful eye at the flat surface and again thought uncomfortably of trout fishing.

Mason sat next to Mercer in the lead guard boat. The morning sun highlighted his advancing age and it was at this moment when the surface party-guy faded away. The relaxed and easy facade had been replaced with Catholic reverence; the ritual was sacred.

The swimmers were lined up on the dock of the boat, and now they were awaiting only Mason's signal.

There would be no starter's pistol, he explained. No sense drawing undue attention so early on.

"Are there any last questions?" Mason asked, his measured tone carrying with unearthly clarity over the flat ocean.

The swimmers got into position. Kurt and Amber both assumed athletic starter's positions. Surfer Dude popped his knuckles and windmilled his arms. Stephen glanced to either side with the expression of a man who was suddenly doubting his decisions.

It was one thing to swim in unfamiliar water – to not know what might be lurking in the murky depths ––it is considered foolish for a diver or swimmer to do so; it was quite another thing when you *know* the monsters are there.

In the lead boat, Mason raised his hand. He paused on the moment.

There was a beat of silence, then a shout from the Surfer Dude: "Hey Mason! Can we start this thing so I can get my money?"

Mason's chiseled features cracked the barest smile, stern at the interruption, yet still pleased at his swimmer's spirit. Mason pointed to the peaks of the nearest island. "There is the Green, ladies and gentlemen," he said. "The lighthouse. Fourteen miles, day one. Twenty miles around the islands on day two. Fourteen miles back to the boat on day three. The prize is one million dollars."

He dropped his other hand.

"The word," he said, "is given."

As one, the four swimmers leaped from the boat into the icy waters of the Pacific, and this year's Contest was on.

CHAPTER 6

The shocking cold of the ocean prompted an immediate, adrenaline-assisted sprint for the first forty or fifty yards – fear was always present, even in the most seasoned of athletes, and the stakes on this day were much higher than even Olympic medals. The rush from the start broke off fairly quickly, and fairly typically, into the pattern it would follow for the rest of the day, establishing early on, as all races do, its 'working order.'

Kurt Wagner had predictably emerged with an early and wide-open lead, his Olympic-winning stroke coasting him comfortably ahead of the rest.

Kurt was actually going against Mason's advice, in stretching out into the early lead. Over the years, Mason had taken the pertinent note that a big lead isn't necessarily a good thing in the Farallons race – you lose the protection of the group. Seals are almost always hit by the sharks when they are swimming alone.

As aware of the danger as anyone, Kurt was taking a calculated risk... and it could be said his strategy was a bit ruthless - something Mason, of course, approved of; this hard streak in Kurt was one of the things that had made him 'right.'

Kurt's strategy was to draw out the field, pulling the others out of the safety of the group as well as they tried to catch him. There was the accommodating fact that his own smooth stroke would draw far less attention than that of his opponents.

The first of the group on Kurt's tail was the Surfer Dude, who was making up in sheer determination and physical effort what he lacked in style. The Surfer Dude was a comparable athlete, but lacked Kurt's specialized training; Surf's style was an enthusiastic go-for-broke headlong sprint. It used a lot of energy, but the Surfer Dude had youth to burn.

There was a lot of splashing, however.

Bringing up an ever-more distant third was Stephen Dreyfuss. Winded and arm-weary after the initial rush from the start, Stephen was trying to pace himself but was being hard-pressed by Amber. Stephen was a strong swimmer but he'd learned to swim like a hiker learns to run – he learned to conserve energy, stay afloat, maximize endurance. This need for speed was leaving him exhausted. His shoulders burned like a novice and he found himself winded.

Intelligent enough to recognize the psychosomatic effect of anxiety, Stephen fought the urge to try and catch the two racers ahead of him, while at the same time ignoring Amber pressing behind him. Instead, he focused on his breathing, letting the oxygen fuel his blood and muscles, loosening out his stroke. It helped to think of it as an easy jog or a glide, moving through the water like a stone being skipped.

It also helped to simply think about anything else but the water around him. He had to go someplace else than inside his head to hide from the knowledge of what lived in these islands; that was the flip side of knowing everything – you knew what was really waiting for you in the dark. And Stephen knew that every shark within miles had known the moment they all entered the water – probably even while they waited on the boat.

A shark's sensory equipment is incredibly acute, as well as wide-ranging, able to detect vibrations and impulses for miles. Oceanic whitetips have been known to follow a scent in the ocean over distances of twenty kilometers. Stephen knew all this, just as he knew for a fact that the sharks were there. And soon enough, he knew that one of them would come to investigate – probably a few had passed by in the murk below already.

Stephen turned his goggled eyes down into the dim, cloudy water, trying to pick out any shadows in the gloom, any shapes that separated from the shifting ocean current. They were down there somewhere, his unfortunate knowledge told him, crossing back and forth, out of sight in the dark, outside their periphery, scouting the four swimmers with their senses like a forest full of snipers with high-powered scopes.

It was only a matter of time before one of them would take the bait.

"We do lose *somebody*," Mason had said. "Every time. Every year."

Right now, Stephen thought, his own odds were one in four.

He nearly screamed when Amber's outstretched hand brushed his foot. The young woman's efficient-looking, military style stroke had closed the distance. Stephen nearly choked on water from his aborted scream, knowing he should continue to pace himself.

Instead, pride forced him to swim faster. His heart beat like a steady drum, pulsing in his ears as he fought to recover his distance and to fight down the adrenaline. Beneath him, the ocean remained a dark and empty blue.

They didn't see the first shark for nearly two hours.

CHAPTER 7

The Surfer Dude had decided he was going to by-God catch Kurt Wagner. His pride was sorely wounded bringing up second – it was the sort of thing that had rarely happened in his life; the Surfer Dude was your consummate all-around athlete, name the game, king of the beach. It didn't matter whether it was beach volleyball, full-contact or touch football, or Frisbee-to-the-death, Surf was the superstar. Surfing was just the game that had made him famous, the one he loved... and the thought of losing any kind of swimming event wound him up into a competitive frenzy.

Surf stepped up his pace a notch, feeling the obligatory burn in his shoulders. He smiled into the splashing salty water, knowing Kurt Wagner's shoulders would now have to burn as well. Wagner coasted along ahead, oblivious at the moment to Surf's advance. Surfer Dude set his sights.

There was just the smallest touch of a hangover that added flavor to Surf's blood as he churned the water, but the alcohol only burned the fuel of youth even hotter. He knew Kurt Wagner wasn't hung-over, and that all by itself made him angry – it was almost *cheating*, Surf thought grimly, forcing his pace another notch higher. It made him even angrier that Wagner still had yet to respond to his pressure.

The Surfer Dude had known guys like Kurt Wagner before – famous types like actors and all the stuck-up, pretty rich people that populated parts of LA and Hollywood, and who mingled with the desperate pretty poor, in an uneasy trade of drugs and services. Surf recognized Kurt's type all right. No starch to him, had to cheat in the mother-fuckin' Olympics; mad because his rich friends with their million dollar houses and hundred thousand dollar cars didn't want to talk to him now that he'd gotten his hands dirty. Take any one of these famous types, Surf thought, and that fame made no difference on the beach. There they would learn to respect the King.

Except this particular famous-guy was beating him, and that fact steamed Surf's blood above and beyond all the rest – if he himself had been winning he could have forgiven everything. Now he lowered his head, smiling again as the joy of battle – diluted somewhat by organized competition – rose up in him. If it had been a running race, or a game on land, this is where he would have been talking trash, hooting out loud, intimidating invectives as he began to close the distance.

Up ahead, Kurt suddenly became aware of his opponent's approach and paid Surfer Dude his finest compliment by stepping up his own pace. Surf smirked into the salt water. He had announced his presence with authority and the race was on for real now; he would bury this Olympic hotshot at sea.

From his right, on the guard boat less than a dozen feet away, there came a single but distinct electronic beep.

The cybernetic clone of a mercenary that sat monitoring the small computer screen said out loud into his headset, "I've got one."

There were two more loud beeps before Surf consciously absorbed their significance.

Each of Mason's guard boats were equipped with several pieces of sophisticated field sensory equipment, everything from sonar blips – which might detect anything so long as it was large enough – and an interesting device Mason had once again copped from ideas of researchers. Over the last several years many groups of scientists had started tagging sharks in the Farallons, mostly for purposes concerning movement and migration, and a number of these were fitted with long-lasting electronic location devices. Most of these gadgets operated on simple, and usually very similar technology. Mason's gadget was simply keyed to detect a broad range of signals – it picked up the shark tags with remarkable accuracy.

Of course, the device only worked on sharks that had already been tagged, but as Stephen Dreyfuss' own research had proved, a lot of the same, tagged sharks were back every year.

And one of them was circling the area now.

The sonar beeped a moment later, offering confirmation.

The guard-boats were communicating with each other via their headsets. The cyborg-merc in Surf's boat was doing most of the talking. His second, black-bearded but otherwise the cyborg's twin, was standing in the boat, scanning the ocean surface, the slim-looking shark-stick held ready.

"It's close," Cyborg said. "I'm trying to pinpoint."

In the water, Surfer Dude could hear the electronic replies from the other boats. "Nothing here," a static-blurred voice barked out. There were similar replies from the two other boats.

Which meant, Surfer Dude realized, that whatever had entered the area had focused in on him.

An odd thought occurred to him at just that moment – and for a wonder it was the first time this particular thought had; he had always crowed the fact that despite all the white sharks out there, an attack on a human was so rare as to be a freak occurrence… yet he himself had been hit twice.

If he really was beating Las Vegas odds in getting attacked at all, let alone more than once, then maybe it was rigged. Maybe there was something about *him*, something subtle in his innate, natural movements that generated those signals the shark wanted to see – a peculiar weakness similar to an allergy to bees, that attracted them like a lure. Surely, there was *something* – a good gambler would bet on it.

Which brought Surfer Dude around to the possibility that maybe this was the quality Mason had seen in him.

In the guard boat the bearded clone suddenly spoke up: "I've got a visual."

Surfer Dude heard the words, spoken as flatly and calmly as he would expect from anyone who was safe in a boat. Surfer Dude had lived on fear and adrenaline his whole life, in fact he felt a certain contempt for those who shied away from the rush. The rush of fear was like whiskey – intoxicating and a motivator. In Surf's head, it brought focus. This time, however, was different.

Something was wrong. Perhaps Mason had managed a psyche job on him after all. For whatever reason the fear wasn't burning right – it was loose, like a faulty wire that sent jolts and surges instead of a controlled flow that could be put to work. Surfer Dude was suddenly conscious of his own splashing.

All four guard-boats had pulled within ten feet of their charges. Stephen Dreyfuss was bobbing his head up and down in the water – looking unfortunately like a small seal – scanning both the surface and the murky depths below. Amber swam steadily, mindful of the conversations going on in the guard boats. Ahead, Kurt had smoothed out his own stroke, turning from side to side, checking his parameters.

Surfer Dude leaned into his stroke, duplicating the same movement, checking first over his right shoulder and then his left. As he turned into the movement, he found himself staring at a dorsal fin knifing the water not ten feet away, pacing him on the left.

"Repeat," the bearded clone said, "I've got a visual." A chuckle. "Oh yeah. It's checkin' him out good."

In the water, Surfer Dude felt the invasive touch of fear, fear of a type that transcended mere danger – there crept into his gut the cold clamminess of dread.

The shark was a big one, probably a sixteen-footer or bigger – typical for shark season in the Farallons. It cruised casually beside, as inoffensive as a dolphin, seemingly uninterested, and Surfer Dude forced himself into a smooth side stroke, dipping his eyes below the surface, watching through his goggles as the shark slipped silently past.

Surf's heart was hammering in his chest as he recalled his own counsel; they aren't interested in us – and more prophetically – if he wanted me, I was his. Surf looked up at the guard boat doubtfully. Both mercs were standing now, prepared to pull him from the water at his word.

The shark had cruised on by and, up ahead, Kurt Wagner stopped, turning as the fin dipped below the surface in the water behind him.

"I've lost visual," Cyborg said. "It's sounded."

Kurt's guardsmen were standing in their boat now as well, scanning the surface.

And Surfer Dude felt *something* – a niggling tremor in his gut. A spider-sense, maybe. He looked down into the water beneath him. Rising up, smoothly, mouth ever so slightly agape, was the shark.

The full import took maybe half a second. Then he launched himself at the guard boat, screaming and inhaling water. "It's coming!" he blurted through a strangling mouthful of seawater. His hands flailed and banged hard against the guard boat's metal rim.

"Get me out of here!" he shouted. Around them, the other guard boats were gathering up the rest of the swimmers – an actual attack was a free 'Out' – but Surf's handlers seemed woefully slow. The bearded clone was reaching for him with all the syrupy slowness of a dream. His cyborg twin had raised Mason's video camera, ready to record next year's highlights.

Surfer Dude screamed in outrage, thrashing towards the boat and he felt his hand caught firmly in the clone's vice-like grip. Then he was hauled bodily out of the water into the boat. He rolled in sudden exhaustion onto the metal floor, choking on half a lung of ocean. There was the sudden spark of electricity as the merc stabbed the Shark Stick in the water. A second later there was a heavy thump as the boat was struck from below.

It was a soft thump. Half-hearted really.

"It didn't go for him," Cyborg said into his headset. "It veered off even without the Stick."

Cyborg lowered the camera and stared down at Surfer Dude in the bottom of his boat. The look in his sun-visored eyes might have been contempt, or hostility – or worse it might have been simple brutal coldness.

"Yeah," Cyborg said, setting the camera aside, speaking again into the headset. "Yeah, he's all right."

Fifteen minutes were allowed after an incident, during which the swimmers were transported an equal but safe distance away. And when those fifteen minutes were up, the swimmers were obligated to go back in.

"This high prey environment,'" Stephen Dreyfuss said as they waited out their time limit, "it makes them excitable. But they know we're not seals - it didn't go for him. It veered off at the last second."

It was a measure of comfort. When time was up, Dreyfuss, along with Kurt and Amber, re-entered the water without undue complaint. Surfer Dude, however, found himself staring down at the water's surface with an unnatural reluctance. Human weakness was not something he'd allowed himself in his life, and he was appalled to discover a previously unsuspected reservoir of fear.

"Time's up," the Cyborg clone said. "You're moving into your first Out."

Surfer Dude stared back at him, then turned and prepared to re-enter the race. He put one foot on the rocking metal edge...

... and his nerves retained the memory of the heavy thumping from below, reverberating in the metal of the boat as the shark nosed around mere inches beneath – nosing around for *him*, the morsel that had suddenly disappeared.

The Cyborg started the boat. From here on, he would begin losing distance as well as time. They puttered back past Dreyfuss and Amber, who were neck and neck, and still a mile behind Kurt. The Cyborg counted Out number two.

The Surfer Dude sat down in the boat, and in that small moment, some of the daredevil went out of him. He didn't need Mason's money - not that badly. The sharks here were different. They... *wanted* you here.

Over the speakers, Mason's outraged voice shouted out in a rant. "*That's* why I don't let his type in!" The Cyborg held up the radio for Surf to hear. "Did you hear me, you cowardly piece of shit?"

Surfer Dude, Mick O'Brien, hung his head. He turned away as the Cyborg counted out his last warning and he became this year's first elimination.

CHAPTER 8

They finished the remainder of the race's first stage without further incident. Kurt maintained an easy lead, reaching the lighthouse beach at half-past three, with Stephen and Amber coming in at four o'clock and four-ten respectively. Stephen struggled out of the surf and lay down, exhausted, on the rocky beach; he was still there as Amber came in shortly behind, striding out of the water as if the fourteen miles were nothing but another afternoon on the lake. Stephen eyed her. He had finished ahead of her today, but his age was showing early.

Kurt had already set up camp. Mason's mercs had set up tents and provided them with a small bonfire. Mercer and two of his men – both the bearded clone and the cyborg from the Surfer Dude's boat – stood guard over their small, open area of beach. All three mercs were additionally armed with high-powered hunting rifles; the big elephant seal bulls sometimes took exception to humans sharing their beach. A large and belligerent elephant seal was no joke and it often took several shots to put one down.

The guards were present for another reason as well. More than once in the Contest's history, one or another of the competitors had tried to eliminate the opposition themselves. There were seven digits at stake and Mason associated with people who would kill for a twenty-cent tip – he didn't want anyone fucking up his Contest. It was his Christmas.

And like a reverent minister, Mason was big on tradition. He had a ceremony on the beach, where he awarded Kurt Wagner the 'Yellow Flag' as the stage leader. He sat there in his chair, staring solemnly, very, very serious as he handed Kurt the flag, instructing Kurt to raise it over his tent during the night.

"Yellow Flag?" Stephen asked as Mason shook his own hand, and then Amber's, for completing the first stage. "Like the stage leader in the Tour de France?"

Mason smiled. "As in 'yum-yum yellow' – the color that sharks like best."

Kurt cast a casually baleful eye in Stephen's direction as he positioned his flag above the tent. "Had to ask, didn't you?" He propped the flag steady and sat down on the rocks.

Mason regarded the three of them, the three remaining contestants, with dutiful respect. "My friends," he said, "I congratulate you all for completing stage one. One little Indian has already run away. And then there were three." Mason's grin was genuine, as cold and shark like as it might be; this was as close to happy as a man like Mason could be. "Rest up for tomorrow. And stay safe tonight." The Carcharodon grin widened again. "My men will watch you... so you don't have to watch each other."

Mason tipped a wink. The sun had dipped into the last of its arc, beginning its slow immersion into the sea; the glare cast shadows in the holes of Mason's eyes. Like a shark, they were black circles and nothing more.

"Look at each other closely tonight, my friends," Mason said. Mercer had left his post and stepped behind Mason's chair. Together, Mercer and a red-pelted version of the same gene experiment that produced the rest of his men, hoisted Mason into his boat. Mercer joined Mason on board and Red-beard took Mercer's post on the beach. The boat's motor fired up.

"Good night, my friends," Mason said above the motor, and Mercer veered the boat out to sea, towards Mason's yacht. In the growing darkness, they faded quickly from sight. The noise of the motor was drowned by the surf.

Red-beard joined the Cyborg and the bearded clone up on the surrounding rocks, the three of them standing like totems in the fading light, staring down over the meager campsite. They seemed not to even move, looking deceptively like harmless rocks as evening descended on the Farallons.

The three swimmers settled down to wait out the night. As the last glimmering glow of the sun crept ever lower into the ocean, the far west of the dark sky lit up a brilliant red.

"Red sky at night," Stephen said aloud. "Maybe that's a good sign." He glanced around at his two competitors. He was looking for conversation. Stony silence, however, was his only response.

Kurt was lying on his back in his tent. He held a small penlight and was shining its beam onto the thin fabric of the tent. The tiny moon of brightness was visible from the outside as it darted in zigzagging patterns across the tent flaps.

Amber was just sitting down after spending the last half-hour some distance down the rocky beach – always under the watch of Mason's guards – they didn't want her running afoul of any bad tempered seals that might come investigating the strange apes that had set camp on their mating grounds. Their honking bleats still sounded in the near distance, although they had quieted with the setting of the sun.

Stephen watched Amber as she settled in around the fire. She held her eyes deliberately low, avoiding eye-contact like the opposite sides of a magnet. The cast of her eyes was even more striking in the dim, sultry fire light, but it brought out other features as well – her eyes were hard and corrupted and stared out of a face that was used to the dark.

So, what had brought her into Mason's contest? Stephen knew his own story, and Kurt's. He even knew the Surfer Dude's story – or rather his lack of one – but Amber was still an unknown quantity. He had the sense that was unusual. As Amber warmed her hands, pointedly on the opposite side of the fire, Stephen speculated on what could have brought *any* pretty young girl into Mason's clutches. Of course, Amber wasn't like the brain-dead sexual creatures Mason employed for his parties; for one thing she was clearly a toughed athlete – she had certainly given Stephen a race today. Neither did she possess the sly, alley cat's eyes of that Alex-bimbo Mason kept on the boat; instead Amber's eyes were clear and intelligent.

There was, however, an undercurrent of anger that Stephen sensed about her. Perhaps it was that anger that kept the corruption from being complete. She sat down on the rocks in front of her tent, her eyes still cast deliberately down. Stephen shrugged, stood up and walked over, sitting down on the rocks next to her.

Amber stood without a word and walked over to the other side of the fire and sat down. Inside his tent, Kurt chuckled.

Kurt tired of tracing patterns on his tent and turned the beam of the pen light into the eyes of Mason's three guards. He shined the surprisingly bright beam into the iris of the first one and then the other, blinking the beam on and off. Mason's men didn't react at all, except to drop their sun visors down until Kurt tired of the game.

Stephen frowned. "I don't think that's such a good idea," he said. "These guys have guns you know."

Kurt leveled the tiny spotlight steadily on Red-beard's right eye. "I think," Kurt said, "if any one of these guys laid a finger on me, they know Mason would turn them into fish food, probably one pliers-twist at a time. It would fuck up the Contest."

"I'm not talking just about Mason," Stephen said. "There's also the fact that you're pissing off the guys that are supposed to be pulling you – us – out of the water before something bites our asses off."

Kurt blinked the light over to the Cyborg, who reacted not at all. "Oh," Kurt said, "I doubt if they would get me out of the water all that fast anyhow. They sure didn't pull the Surfer Dude out that fast today." He glanced confidentially in Stephen's direction. "You see, Mason needs highlights. And no one's been eaten yet."

"He's right."

There was a momentary pause as Kurt and Stephen realized it was Amber who had spoken. She was looking at them directly for the first time since they'd come into her acquaintance. Her eyes were even more striking head on, mirrored in the firelight, but like still water, it was hard to tell their depths.

"What do you mean, 'he's right'?" Stephen asked. "Who are you anyway?"

Amber glared back with the mistrustful eyes of youth that had seen too much, and was determined not to be taken. Her suspicious hostility was not blunted by her unnerving cynicism; in the crackling of the fire and the surrounding dark, her words were also something less than optimistic.

"I mean that if a shark comes at one of us tomorrow, Mason won't pull us out. Not before one of us is eaten. One of us each year, he said. That's a guarantee. And all our odds just dropped down to one in three." Amber kicked at a stone and rolled it into the fire. "The Contest is rigged," she said. "The whole point is Mason wants to watch us die."

"How would you know what Mason wants?" Stephen asked. He numbered over some of his previous suppositions on the subject and could find nothing good.

Kurt focused on the practical. "What do you mean the Contest is rigged?"

Amber smiled thinly. "I mean he'll do everything he can to make sure we die. I'm serious. He gets off on it. It's the only thing that gets him off anymore." Amber stopped suddenly, as if afraid she'd said too much. Kurt, however, was quick to pounce.

"What are you?" he asked. "One of his bimbos?" Kurt blinked his penlight in her eyes, turning away her glare. He pressed easily. "Well?" he asked. "What's your story? How do I know you're not just full of shit like everybody else?"

Amber's eyes narrowed, a spark of anger momentarily lighting her face, but then Stephen saw the cool visor she commonly wore instead of an expression drop quickly back down over her face. She turned back to the fire, sighing deeply as she reestablished her distance. When she spoke, her voice was composed.

"Mason's had dealings with my family," she said. "Specifically, he's had dealings with my brother, who was really the only family I've had since I was seventeen."

Now that her visor was up, she could meet the two men's eyes directly. "My brother, Denny, was a smack head. Mason deals a little heroin. Denny ran up some debts. Mason was about to collect out of his hide when I stepped in."

Amber shifted uncomfortably on the rocks. "I assumed the debt," she said.

Kurt nodded. Stephen, inexperienced in street matters, waited for the explanation.

"I got the money together. I sold my car, my house, took out a loan for more at the bank. Turned out it didn't matter anyway. See, the moment Denny was in the clear, he ran right back to his same old suppliers and ran those debts right back up again. They killed him six weeks later. Either that or he overdosed with extreme suicide on his mind and two broken thumbs."

Amber kicked another rock angrily into the fire. "That didn't change the debt though," she said. "Mason still wanted his money. And I was out of resources. Which was maybe what Mason had in mind all along. It wasn't too long before he offered to put me to work."

"Put you to work?" Stephen asked, a touch slow on the uptake. "What does that mean?" Kurt bounced a pebble off his head and speared him with his penlight.

Amber ignored Stephen – by now it was habit. "It wouldn't be the brothels, Mason told me. He emphasized that I would be used for special clients only."

Kurt gave Amber a cynical once over. "What makes you so special?" he asked.

Amber glared darts in Kurt's direction. "I guess he just liked me."

"Is that why he let you in the Contest?" Kurt asked. "He must like you a lot."

"I guess," Amber said coolly.

"So what makes you think the Contest is rigged?" Kurt wanted to know. "I mean so far you told us that Mason's a 'mean guy.' Well, no shit. I saw that on the news."

Amber shook her head. "You know, but you don't *know*. The first thing he did when I assumed my brother's debt, was make me sit through a screening of his little video show. All the time he's talking to me like he's Father Callahan or something – hopping around on his one fucking leg." She kicked at another stone.

"He loves that shit," she went on. "And I don't suppose it occurred to either of you that there were a hell of a lot more clips than he could have recorded in just fourteen years of races. It would have had to have been more like fifty."

Stephen and Kurt looked steadily at Amber and she had their full attention. The bonfire ruined their night vision and all around them was black, the ocean invisible. Amber's eyes were dark, and the reflective sheen may have been tears from the smoke – or, Stephen thought, cold metal beneath the surface.

"There were," Stephen allowed, "a lot of clips in that video."

"I think," Kurt ventured, "that Mason meant what he said about the shark-attack stats in southern California."

Amber smiled her thin, humorless smile. "Most serial murderers don't have money," she said. "Mason's a good example of what happens when one does. He doesn't have this Contest so somebody can *win*."

"So why are you here, then?" Kurt asked. "Why do it then?"

Amber shrugged. "Because somebody gets to win. And if you win, he'll pay you – no bullshit. Because it's better if you're running towards something, salvation maybe. He wants us to run hard, so he gives both the carrot *and* the stick. And it doesn't matter to me that the carrot is only there to keep a dead man fighting a little longer, it's still there."

Amber's voice had roughened, emotion threatening the integrity of her icy visor. Stephen thought he saw a tremble in her arms. He thought it was fear, but when she spoke again, her voice had taken on the ugly grate of anger. The sheen in her eyes had thickened to real tears. They showed nothing soft, however.

"Why am I here?" Amber looked hard at Kurt and Stephen together. "I'll tell you why. My life turned to shit – just like yours did. And this is a chance. My last fucking chance. And I hate both of you for being in my way."

She suddenly, violently, grabbed a small piece of driftwood and pitched it hard into the fire. Sparks kicked up and Stephen yelped as one touched down on his neck. On the encroaching rocks behind them, their guardsmen perked to attention. Amber stood, glaring down at Stephen and Kurt, and her hate certainly seemed to be genuine.

"I'm not stupid," she said. "I know I can't beat either of you in a straight race. The only way I can win is if both of you are eliminated. And I hope you are."

And with that, she turned an about-face and strode away from them down the dark, rocky beach. One of Mason's guards, the Red-bearded one Kurt had started calling 'Leprechaun,' separated from the others and followed, staying within a protective distance – there were still the honks and barks of seals in the near dark. Back at the fire, both Stephen and Kurt stared after her as she became indistinct in the blackness.

Kurt was shaking his head. "Man. Damaged goods. Do not accept." He tipped a despairing eye at Stephen. "And you wanted to fuck her last night on the boat."

Stephen shrugged. "I thought I might get eaten today."

"Trust me," Kurt said rolling on his back, "you don't want any part of that woman. She's more carnivorous than that blond Alex-bitch Mason keeps as a pet. Totally fucked in the head." He was twirling his penlight on his tent canvas again.

Stephen looked after Amber's departing buttocks, which despite their owner's less than sunny disposition, remained a pleasing and remarkable sight.

"I'd actually like to make up my own opinion, if you don't mind," Stephen said. He frowned at Kurt. "What is it with you anyway? Are *all* women fucked?"

"No," Kurt said, tracing patterns, "just the ones I've met lately." He nodded in Amber's direction. "Certainly *that* one," he said.

"She did," Stephen reflected, "just say she hoped both of us get eaten tomorrow." Stephen looked at Kurt. "What about you?" he asked. "Are you hoping we get killed?"

Kurt smiled. "I don't have to. It's like Amber said. Neither of you can beat me in a straight race. I just have to hope I don't get eaten."

With that, Kurt switched off his penlight and rolled over in his tent, apparently right to sleep, because he said nothing else. Stephen turned to the ocean. The steady crash of the waves against the rocks was much different than the smooth purr of the boat's engine the night before. Stephen listened as the immense, inexorable weight of the tide battered the land, and he found himself feeling a bit small – small and insignificant before nature.

That was good. He wanted to be small. Unnoticeable. He wanted to slip through these islands as anonymously as the tide tossing a grain of sand.

He heard his own voice in his head: every shark in the area knows the moment you enter the water.

And of course, Mason had apparently been keeping them fed. Stephen looked out on the dark ocean and thought of Sandy - a massive, powerful, aggressive representation of her species. A giant fish Stephen had almost come to care for as a pet. He wondered if she was out there now. She had never missed a seal season yet.

Stephen sat up for a while and watched the ocean, glancing occasionally down the beach to see if Amber was coming back. He could see her guardsman standing on an outcropping of rocks. Presumably, Amber was hunkered down among them, perhaps bedding down for the night. Stephen gave up and climbed into his tent.

As he lay down, he wondered if he was like Amber. Because Kurt was right - Stephen knew he couldn't beat an Olympic champion in a swimming race. Did that mean he was hoping Kurt would be – to coin Amber's phrase – 'eliminated'?

The question kept sleep at bay for a long time, but eventually his physical exhaustion took over and he slept, albeit fitfully and unresolved.

And miles off shore, the lights of Mason's yacht flashed like a beacon in the darkness.

On board, Mason was deciding how to deal with this year's first elimination.

CHAPTER 9

"I've never been scared before," the Surfer Dude said. Alex, who had been his supportive ear for most of the afternoon, stifled a yawn, forcing understanding from her drooping eyes; the Surfer Dude had started repeating himself fairly early on. She was, however, stuck with him until Mason returned from his ceremony on the beach. It was just the two of them on the yacht and Alex, taking advantage of the opportunity and the obvious physical chemistry, had fucked him almost right away, hoping he would simply shut up and fall asleep afterwards. No such luck.

Truth to tell, the fuck had actually served to open him up even more. The fuck had revealed to Alex a fundamental change that had occurred in the famous California Surfer Dude – perhaps a permanent one. He had fucked her for comfort, and had done so like a nervous teen-aged boy. There was no sense of masculine conquest, nor really even the good-natured gusto that Alex would have expected. Afterwards he clung to her and gushed like a sixteen year-old girl on the telephone.

Alex listened patiently - listening to men's bullshit was what she mostly did for a living. Aside from the tedious chore of occasionally spreading her legs, she might as well have been a psychiatrist. This was true of most women in her line of work, particularly the smart ones, and Alex played the head-shrinker quite well. She stroked the Surfer Dude's long blond locks, and her fingers were surely as soothing and soft as had been Delilah's on Samson. Unlike Delilah, Alex felt no direct responsibility for the Surfer Dude's ruin.

And ruin was truly what it was. This was never illustrated more clearly than the moment he took a lock of his own hair, tugging at it wearily. "I should cut it. I'm getting a little old to be walking around looking like David Lee Roth."

"So is he," Alex remarked. But she played with his tousled mop of hair, running her fingers through it deliciously. "Still," she said, "it'd be a shame to lose all this. I can't imagine the California Surfer Dude without his mop."

The Surfer Dude didn't smile. He breathed a heavy sigh. "Don't call me that," he said. "My name's Mick. No one calls me that anymore. Not for years. I think my mother was the last one."

Alex knew through Mason that the Surfer Dude's mother had died when he was sixteen. If she had not known, he had supplied the information himself several times during the evening. Alex suppressed her own heavy sigh, blinking her eyes attentively.

Still, there was a certain poignancy as the Surfer Dude struggled to deal with the sudden change in himself. The Surfer Dude – Mick O'Brien – was the one contestant that stirred Alex's own painful memories. In that way, they were kin. That might have been another reason she fucked him; it was something nice to do.

The Surfer Dude hadn't been scared of anything, Alex thought, but Mick O'Brien was another story. Alex found herself sympathizing and associating; like her, he was more or less alone in the world – and today, when he discovered fear, he had lost the hustle that he had always relied on to get him by.

Alex was preparing herself for another round of stories and grade-school philosophies, but the Surfer Dude – Mick – had fallen silent. He lay with his head in her lap, clinging childlike to her legs. And like a child, he soon fell into a light doze. Alex stroked his hair until it deepened into true sleep.

Mason would be arriving home soon. It would be best if she were dressed when he got here – at least in a robe. As she slipped her legs out from under the Surfer Dude's sleeping head, propping it up with a pillow, she heard the distant purr of Mason's boat. She moved quietly, glancing back at the Surfer Dude who was beginning to snore. She paused for a moment before retiring to her own quarters.

Best to just let him sleep, Alex thought.

Mason would be wanting words with him when he awoke.

CHAPTER 10

The Surfer Dude, who was thinking of himself as Mick O'Brien for the first time in years, wasn't sure how long he slept. He came awake with a start some indeterminate time later to find himself alone in the darkened cabin. Alex had apparently left him for her own quarters. He missed her comforting warmth; her absence had left a cold spot beside him.

He wondered if Mason was back yet.

Mason was angry with him, and had made no pretense about it. As yet, however, Mason had been occupied and the Surfer Dude had so far been spared direct confrontation. Of course, that was probably too good to last. Mason didn't like quitters. He had broached the Surfer Dude on this very topic when he'd originally interviewed him as a potential contestant.

Mason had been direct. "I don't like your type," he had said. "All this foolish reckless bullshit – it's nothing but adrenaline, not courage. I was young once too." He had indicated his missing leg, meeting the Surfer Dude's eye with zero levity. "A roller coaster moves too fast to chicken out. I think if your type has time to think then maybe you're not so brave after all. My Contest is a test of nerves, Mr. O'Brien. If you get into a tight spot out there, you won't be in the middle of an adrenaline rush. I think you might quit."

The Surfer Dude, with the prospect of a million dollars dangling before him, all for a measly fifty-mile swim, had assured Mason, with utter arrogant confidence, that he had never quit anything in his life.

Well, he had now. And Mason wasn't happy.

And come to think of it, the fact that he had just fucked Mason's girlfriend probably wouldn't help his cause either.

In retrospect, that last part seemed pretty stupid. How had he actually let that happen? Alex was hot and all, but Surf had never suffered for the attention of the ladies – Baywatch beauties every one of them; the simple fact was that he hadn't wanted to be alone. He had needed something badly and Alex had been right there to give it. Looking at it that way, it wasn't really even his fault. Surf wondered for a moment about Alex's own motivations.

He rose stiffly from the couch, feeling his way in the dark up the stairs to the main deck. He padded noiselessly up the steps, feeling the cool night breeze greet him. The boat lights were dark, like it had been when Mason had ordered lights out on the eve of the race. Mason must have already returned, perhaps he had simply retired to his quarters with Alex, choosing to ignore the Surfer Dude altogether. Surf was fine with that: a Colin Mason ass-chewing was something he didn't relish the thought of – there had been stories.

Surfer Dude was beginning to relax, wondering now if Mason intended to make him wait out the remainder of the race before taking him back to shore. When Mason suddenly spoke in the dark behind him, Surf nearly shouted out loud.

"Come over here, Mr. O'Brien," Mason said.

Mason was sitting there silently in the dark. His chair was pushed up to the railing near the lowest point on deck – the very place he had started them off that morning. Mercer stood at Mason's shoulder and their attention was on the water beyond. Surfer Dude looked down at the obsidian-black ocean and could see nothing but the dancing reflection of the moon. Then the foul smell reached his nostrils.

Mercer dipped a ladle into a bucket of fish guts and splashed the rank mixture into the water. The two of them were chumming.

And at just that moment it seemed that the reflection of the moon was broken by a dark, darting shape just under the surface. When Mason spoke again it seemed that the cool measured tones were like a similar shadow that skittered past the Surfer Dude's heart. This new and unpleasant emotion of fear rose up once again.

"It's hard to coax them out at night," Mason said, indicating the dark, torpedo-like shapes that remained just out of clear view in the water below. "Surface predators are mostly inactive at night. The surface is mostly invisible." Mason turned a baleful eye over his shoulder. "But they are still there. They don't sleep and they can follow their nose." Mason's lips turned up into his humorless smile. "They'll still follow blood."

The Surfer Dude said nothing. He regarded Mason and, for the first time, it occurred to him that this guy was crazy. Really crazy – not wild, not reckless, but the kind of vicious, truly sadistic way that makes human monsters. It occurred to the Surfer Dude for the first time that Mason might be about to throw him to the sharks.

Alex, Surf thought – the bitch must have ratted him out. He began scrambling in his mind for apologies. Mason, however, dealt with first things first.

"You fucked up my race, Mr. O'Brien," Mason said flatly. The words were judgment, and were not up for discussion. Behind Mason, Mercer turned his attention from his ladling – with Mason's weird sense of ritual, it would fall to Mercer to act as the executor of the sentencing phase of Mason's judgment. Translation: he would be the one who would actually be throwing the accused overboard. Surfer Dude, who had lost precious few fights in his life, sized Mercer up with unprecedented reluctance.

The fucking guy could kill him, Surf realized, staring wide-eyed with something like panic. It was the same unmanning feeling that had come upon him in the race, the moment he had seen the ascending shadow of the shark, moving up at him out of the murk. And the cybernetic attachments that passed for Mercer's eyes were every bit as dark and dead as the lifeless doll eyes of the shark.

"Listen," Surf said, "I'm sorry about the race. I mean, I choked. I swear that's never happened to me before."

Mason turned fully from the ocean for the first time. "You were afraid," he said.

"Well... yeah."

"I suppose," Mason said, the stern glare in his eyes softening for a moment, "that is the point of my race. I said it was a test of nerve. An ultimate test of nerve." He regarded the Surfer Dude with sorry contempt. "I suppose it's not your fault that you're sadly lacking."

Surf knew better than to object. He hung his head dutifully. Mason measured him tiredly.

"And I suppose," Mason continued," I should have known better. In a way, it's my fault for letting sorry beach trash like you into my Contest in the first place. You just behaved according to your own sniveling, greedy, cowardly nature." Mason smiled a little. "Once again – my fault. I misjudged you when I thought I saw something more to you than that."

The Surfer Dude stood there like a scolded puppy, but inside he actually saw a glimmer of hope.

"However," Mason said, "that's not what worries me."

Surf stared back blankly.

Mason smiled, shaking his head regretfully. "You see, the thing is, if I did misjudge you, then maybe I was wrong to think I could trust you." Mason's eyes grew distant and thoughtful. "I wonder if you can really be trusted to keep your mouth shut about participating in my race."

The Surfer Dude started to object, started to stammer out a reply, an assurance – of course, he wouldn't say anything, of course, he wouldn't tell – but then Mercer was moving forward. Adrenaline surging, the Surfer Dude stepped up to fight, but his swinging fist was snatched out of the air. In the blink of an eye, his arm was twisted and creaking behind his back. He screeched in sudden pain. Mercer wrestled him over to the railing, bending him over the top bar, forcing his face over the side.

Surf could see his own reflection. The boat's subsurface lights came on and now he could see the reddish glow of the chum-filled water. There were the hints of torpedo shapes just outside the reach of the light. Somewhere, Surf knew, a camera was switching on.

"Mason, listen," Surfer Dude blurted, almost involuntarily. "Don't do this. I swear to God you can trust me." He started to say more but Mercer silenced him by pressing the ten-inch blade of his skinning knife flush against Surf's throat. Surf's breath stopped, his heart hammering as Mercer turned the blade ever so slightly into his skin.

"Mason," Surf whispered, "please…"

Mason smiled. "Now *that's* a knife!" he said good-naturedly.

Tears began to blur the Surfer Dude's eyes, running down the side of his face, and he felt the touch of shame that battled for a moment with the pinch of fear. He had last cried when his mother had died, nearly seven years ago now. But that had been grief. It hadn't reduced him. But he felt diminished now; the tears began to fall harder. When he tried to speak again, his pleading voice was little more than a choke.

"Mason, I swear. I swear I won't tell," he said.

And Mason raised his hand.

The knife blade miraculously vanished from the Surfer Dude's throat and Mercer suddenly yanked him back over the railing, back on board, setting him back on his trembling bare feet. Unable to believe, the Surfer Dude wiped savagely at his tears, turning to Mason in groveling thanks.

"You won't regret it, Mr. Mason," he babbled, gushing with all the earnestness of an altar-boy. "I swear on my life."

Mason nodded to Mercer. Mercer brought the blade of the skinning knife fast and hard across the back of the Surfer Dude's legs, severing the hamstrings to the bone. Terminal arterial blood squirted like a fire hydrant. Surf's squealing was like that of a pig in mid-butcher.

"What are you doing?!" he screamed, in outrage and betrayal. "I said I wouldn't tell!"

"Oh, I believe you," Mason said easily. "But you fucked my girlfriend."

With that, Mercer flipped Mick O'Brien, formerly known as the California Surfer Dude, into the chum-filled ocean. The protesting scream was abbreviated by the splash and the Surfer Dude found himself swimming in the reddish-tinted water, standing out in the dark in the ship's sub-surface lights. Clouds of his own blood added to the fish guts, pumping from his severed arteries like a broken oil main. He found his legs useless and he struggled to tread water with his arms alone.

The sharks were shy at night – it took a bit of time. But soon enough, there came the first experimental tugs from below, like trout testing a line. The screaming that accompanied these first tentative tugs were recorded for posterity by Mason's cameras. The shrieks were loud and long, mixed with curses and pleading, but when they ended it was sudden and without ceremony; a small splash, a gurgle of water in choked lungs, and the California Surfer Dude was gone.

Up in Mason's cabin, Alex heard the screams – screams of the kind that she had heard before. Mason's cameras would be cranking away. Soon Mason would be bringing this latest home movie back to bed. He would plug it in the VCR and he would make Alex watch it while he fucked her. There would be no trouble for Mason getting off tonight.

Alex shut her eyes and waited for the thump of Mason's one leg on the stairs.

CHAPTER 11

The second day of the race opened without the fanfare of the first. It was a competition at this point, Mason believed, and he didn't want extraneous elements corrupting the integrity of the Contest. Still, he was religiously present, piously offering encouragement to each racer as they warmed up on the beach.

Mason seemed in particularly good humor this morning.

For Amber, that in itself was reason enough for worry.

Amber's stakes in this race were perhaps even deeper than she had let on to her male counterparts the night before – and what was worse was the fact that it looked as if her chances of winning were growing dim. Mason himself had presided over the time clock as each swimmer was allotted their previous day's lead-time. Kurt was first with nearly a thirty-minute head. When Stephen was allowed to begin the stage, Kurt was nearly out of sight. When her own turn had come, just a few excruciating minutes later, Amber had found herself discouraged before she even hit the water.

And Mason's too-jovial demeanor this morning didn't help. In Amber's experience, Mason in good humor rarely came from anything good. Amber had fancied she'd heard screams echoing over the water during the night and she had paused to consider the possible fate of the Surfer Dude. Amber knew that Mason had killed for less.

Nevertheless, Amber pushed it out of her mind, content to dismiss last night's distant howls as merely the wind. She was able to do that by summoning a degree of mental toughness that her association with Mason had enforced upon her – a degree of toughness that was considerable.

Ironically, it was perhaps Mason alone who could have truly appreciated that nth degree, by the simple act of Amber's controlled athletic stroke - not Olympic-level, but certainly an experienced racer - and by the way she bent her head into the waves, committing to the race despite a sea that was rougher than the day before. Mason knew Amber's special terror, which she had battled her whole life; it was a simple childhood fear that had nothing to do with the tough times her life had seen growing up.

Amber had a phobia of deep water, and of the ocean in particular, which stemmed back from when she was no more than a toddler. This was why, as an older child, she had participated in things like swim team, despite an otherwise delinquent youth; her greatest fear she battled head on. She had mostly beaten her fear of lakes, and wasn't bothered at all by pools anymore.

The ocean, however, was another matter. It had been on a San Diego beach, not all that far from the immediate shore, just thirty miles distant; Amber's mother had taken her, along with other mothers and children, for a late summer day at the beach. One of Amber's playmates – it must have been Kindergarten, because Amber remembered the little girl from class – had been grabbed by the undertow and drowned.

Kathy had been the little girl's name, and Amber had not even known her particularly well. At the time of the incident, in fact,

Amber had not really even been all that shook up. Little Kathy had simply disappeared, not to be found for several days and several miles up the beach. At the time, Amber had only really been aware of upset and general chaos among the adults. It wasn't until the little girl's body was found that the two images fused together.

Amber, whose mother had been no angel, learned readily enough that the little girl's face had been eaten away, and it was for this reason that it was a couple of days after Kathy was found that she was positively identified.

That had been the worst of it for Amber. She had been *eaten* after she was dead.

And for Amber, the association was with the ocean, and the image of the rolling, white-capped waves reminded her of giant reaching hands. This had been what had snatched that little girl away, swallowing and drowning her, regurgitating her later, half eaten-and digested, crawling with carrion eaters, her insides moving with worms.

Amber often had dreams afterwards in which her arms and legs were crawling with worms, her own flesh gone sour with rot. That old Hitchcock-theme had given her the creeping horrors: the worms crawl in, the worms crawl out...

And it gave Mason a particular pleasure, Amber knew, to see her swimming in his race. It was the worst thing he could possibly do to her – better than mere murder or rape because it had *duration*... and because it was her own particular terror.

But if she won, Mason would pay. She knew enough about Mason to believe that. And it was that very belief that fed the growing hatred of the two men who were presently much closer to the prize than she was. Amber hadn't been kidding the night before; she wanted this prize, and the simple fact that her best wasn't going to be enough to win it was the final horror. Her life was once again going to be determined by others.

It wasn't a race. Kurt was beyond catching. Stephen as well, perhaps motivated by the race Amber had given him the previous day – and wounded male pride, of course – was stretching out his own lead, doing his best to keep Kurt in sight. Amber focused all her will on the two of them together, trying to hate and resent them as much as she could. Anger was like gasoline – it burned hot and flashy, drawing her attention from older feelings of slowly mounting dread.

Now that the racers were stretched out over distance, there was none of the group defense left. To Amber, the water itself was an icily suffocating, physical manifestation of claustrophobia itself. The very fact of her progress was a testament to her own inner discipline. She supposed it was like some hard-nose psychiatrist's version of a phobia exercise.

Of course, there was also that other little matter of the sharks.

Amber had actually given them little thought, occupied with the more pressing matter of simply breathing and performing in the ocean's clammy cold grip. She knew they were there, though; she hadn't been lying about seeing Mason's unedited home movies. And repeated viewings at that.

In an academic way that she used to fortify her self-discipline, Amber knew that the ocean itself wouldn't hurt you unless you disrespected it. Not so the ocean's predators. And while Amber's specific fear was not sharks, the very fact of having to pay attention for them forced her out of the physical zone she needed to be in to compete.

Of course, she had no idea what she really might do if a triangular dorsal fin were to suddenly appear right beside her. Her own cool head had certainly saved her life more than once. But usually there hadn't been fear to start. Right now, she was wired as tight as an electric guitar, and the guitar string is at its tightest right before it breaks.

And when the first shadows flickered past beneath her, Amber felt the first crank of the over-tightened string. Still, she maintained an admirable poise and restraint.

Her guard-boat that day was piloted by Kurt's redheaded Leprechaun, and a stockier, tattooed anthropoid that probably had at least one human parent. Tattoo also apparently had human-like opposable thumbs, for he steered the boat and monitored the radio. Leprechaun was the cameraman and he held the camcorder – Mason's eye – ever ready for impending highlights. The radio, which was on stand-by, suddenly squawked to life with a distorted voice from one of the other guard-boats.

"I've got movement," the scratchy voice said. "Something's coming in on sonar."

It was then that Amber had first spotted the darting shadows in the murky dimness beneath her. Bizarrely she felt the odd impulse to simply ignore it – to pretend it wasn't there, in effect hiding her head in the sand like a watery ostrich. The adrenaline, however, pumped through her system quite involuntarily, demanding vigorous action. It took all her will to suppress the urge, forcing herself to pause, minimizing her movements, trying to see both above and below the surface at once.

She could see nothing. The waves, however, were a bit higher today – a dorsal fin could be cruising along ten feet away and she might miss it until it was too late. Neither was the visibility much better below. The ocean around her was apparently empty. But she could hear Mason's voice in her mind, reminding her that the sharks were always there. She could also hear Stephen Dreyfuss' voice, explaining scientifically how Great White Sharks were like trout, and how, in the Farallons, they hit and hit hard. She remembered the Surfer Dude laughing and pointing at the TV screens from the safety of Mason's yacht, and then recalled his shrieking wails as he had flailed for his guard-boat as a two-ton, cold-blooded mouthful of teeth had come ascending smoothly from below.

Particularly she remembered Kurt's voice, cynically wise: "Oh I doubt they'd pull me out of the water all that fast anyway."

And of course, there was her own voice: "Mason just wants to watch us die."

The shadows could have been in her mind, Amber admonished herself, physically resisting her own adrenaline, keeping her breathing slow and even. That was when Tattoo spoke for the first time, instructing the Leprechaun to get his camera ready. "I've got something on radar," he said.

Amber's carefully controlled breathing caught like a cold engine. In heroic fashion, she maintained her smooth, rippleless stroke. She did, however, veer herself a touch closer to the guard-boat.

And didn't it seem as if the boat angled itself just a touch further away?

This time the darting shadow below was distinct. Amber could feel the displaced water and had the sense of other shapes moving just out of sight. She turned more directly towards the boat and an indescribable hatred came over her as she saw Tattoo turn the boat another foot or two further away.

The sonar beeped again. Red-haired Leprechaun was grinning, breaking the customary stone-faced visage of his comrades. He evidently enjoyed his job, zooming his camera lens in close for a shot of the expression on Amber's face – Mason liked those. "Smile, honey," the Leprechaun said. Amber heard Kurt's voice again, reminding her that Mason needed highlights.

Then she felt the displacement of water right beside her, something solid touched her leg and her nerve broke.

Amber leaped for the guard-boat with a guttural scream that was half-gargled seawater. She flailed blindly, her careful self-control shattering like safety glass in a windshield, swallowing more water, dragging her hands along the metal rim, but gaining no purchase.

The Leprechaun was grinning, holding his camera. Tattoo extended his hand... but *slowly*, just out of her reach. Amber realized then that they were going to let it happen. They were just going to let her die. Panic took over completely and she was nearly drowning when one of her desperately grasping hands latched onto the side rail of the guard-boat.

After an interminable second, Tattoo finally – finally! – reached over the edge, hauling her, choking and screaming, from the water. Amber lay at the foot of the boat, gagging water, trembling and shaking much as had the Surfer Dude and many others before him. She looked up at her guardsmen and found she didn't have the breath enough to curse.

The two of them, Tattoo and Leprechaun, stared down at her for a moment. Then they both burst into boisterous laughter.

"That was a close call," Tattoo said, his voice an Australian lilt. "Weren't it, Lassie?"

Amber looked over the side and saw what had swam up next to her in the ocean.

The sleek black head of an elephant seal poked curiously through the surface. The seal's eyes seemed amused, even a trifle concerned at the spectacle its innocent investigation of this strange swimming ape had caused.

"That's an Out for ya, Lassie," Tattoo said. "Might as well take the rest. Time's already spent."

Amber blinked, considering; there would be fifteen minutes before she had to resume the race. Beyond that and she would have to spend another Out. Of course, if she waited out the time she would be falling even further behind.

At just that moment, however, she wasn't quite ready to jump back in.

She had about five minutes left in her allotted time when the radio suddenly spoke again.

"Sonar again," the voice squawked. It sounded like Blackbeard, who was the second on Steven's boat about a hundred yards ahead. "Clear signal this time."

A moment later the sonar on Amber's boat beeped aloud.

Leprechaun raised the camera in Amber's direction again. "Say cheese," he said. Amber glared but then realized the camera wasn't focused on her this time. Leprechaun zoomed the camcorder past her shoulder, focusing in on the ocean behind them.

Amber turned and saw the fin tailing the boat, keeping an easy distance of ten feet between them.

Her time clock clicked away another minute.

CHAPTER 12

The shark was immense, dwarfing the fourteen-foot guard-boat. In the Farallons, big female Great Whites often exceeded eighteen feet. And the crescent shaped bite taken out of this one's dorsal fin established its owner's identity right away.

Tattoo spoke into the radio, alerting the other boats. "It's Sandy," he said. "Confirm for Mr. Mason that we've got this year's first sighting of Sandy."

Amber stared back at the dark black shape following the boat; it paced them easily, cruising now off to the side. The scarred fin was a signature, like the villain's black hat. Enter: Darth Vader. Amber knew Sandy's reputation well enough – Mason talked about her more than his mother. It was one thing, however, to know something intellectually, but it was quite another to discover it as a face-to-face reality.

The torpedo shape was moving past them now, as casual and disinterested as a car passing on the freeway. But Amber knew that this was *her* – *the* shark. If ever there was a candidate for the real *Jaws*, Sandy was it.

At over eighteen feet and thick of body, Sandy was the only shark that had been positively identified in multiple, repeat appearances in both Stephen Dreyfuss' documentaries and Colin Mason's own videos.

She was not an animal to trust. No one had told her that humans had supplanted her kind as the world's top predator. To Sandy, humans were just more protein. Kinda nasty tasting even. In Sandy's world, she was absolutely dominant, even among her own kind. Unusually aggressive and as big as the largest Carcharodons on record, Sandy would be mostly unchallenged in the ocean. Even the odd orca might give a white like Sandy some room.

No doubt about it.

Word of Sandy's stage entrance blared on the radios from boat to boat. Sandy herself had sailed past Amber's guard boat and was homing in on where Stephen was still swimming up ahead. At the first beep of sonar, Stephen immediately took his first Out. Dreyfuss knew Sandy personally and he was taking no chances. As his cloned, merc guards hauled him out of the water, Amber heard Stephen's voice over the radio. "That's the thing," he was saying. "She's not unpredictable – you *know* she's going to come after you."

Amber could see Stephen standing in the boat, between seventy-five and a hundred yards ahead. The tailing fin had fallen in tow behind his guard-boat and all three occupants, racer and guards alike, provided their undivided attention. Blackbeard was pilot and he veered the boat off to the side. The fin followed for a moment and then sounded.

Farther ahead, nearly three quarters of a mile, Kurt also elected to take an Out. He had sufficient lead to burn, and was apparently taking seriously his own stated intent he had voiced the night before: simply finish the race alive… don't get eaten. He stood in the boat, staring back in their direction. Amber could barely see him against the sun glare.

Sandy, however, had not resurfaced. Blackbeard's voice barked over the radio. "I've lost visual."

There were still beeps of sonar, however.

Amber's Out-timer beeped a moment later.

Leprechaun smiled at her, visibly enjoying his job more than was common for Mason's mercs. "Time's up, darlin'," he said.

She glared back. If she didn't resume the race immediately, she would be sacrificing her second Out in an hour. One more than that and she would have to stay in no matter what or else forfeit the race. She squinted in the distance after Stephen's boat. Dreyfuss was still standing, scanning the ocean.

"Still nothing," Blackbeard's voice blared over the radio. "And I've lost sonar."

Amber cursed as she signaled to Leprechaun that she was taking her second Out.

Her second Out - fifteen more minutes of waiting, painstakingly slow, yet passing with alarming quickness. Fifteen more minutes of scanning the ocean surface, remembering Mason's little lectures; remembering how Sandy was known to scout out prey from as far as a hundred yards out, then sounding and appearing out of nowhere from below, charging up with the weight of a Black Rhino led by a mouthful of razor teeth.

Yeah, that would be a sight from the water. Probably a real thrill. And Amber was quite sure that even Mason's graphic videos failed to convey the real rush of such an experience. Falling out of a skyscraper window might feel something like that.

Mason loved this part, Amber knew, and at the very thought of it she was overcome with an utter loathing; it was *this* that Mason wanted. Above all, it was this. It was that gut fear that Mason wanted driven into you. He wanted to see that point where you break. It wasn't the *best* part, but it was in the top two.

The best part, of course – Amber had no illusions – was when Sandy got you.

Amber watched Stephen up ahead, wondering if he would employ a second Out of his own. If he passed, it might provide him an opportunity to cut down some of Kurt's lead. Amber herself hoped Stephen would pass – that would mean he would have to enter the water first. If Stephen did take another break, Kurt probably would too, which left Amber the choice of entering first or squandering her last Out.

"What do you think, guys?" Stephen's voice said over the radio. "Is she gone?" Amber wasn't sure who he was talking to... the merc guards on the boat with him? Or perhaps he was speaking to the rest of them through the radio. More likely, he was just vocalizing out loud to himself.

"Sandy's not a girl to trust," Stephen's voice said. "I've seen it a hundred times. If she's interested, she'll be back around." Stephen let out a nervous chuckle. "Let's hope she knows we're not elephant seals."

Not, Amber thought, that it had seemed to matter much to Sandy in the past; she had, after all made as many appearances, if not more, in Mason's videos as Stephen's. In the Farallons at least, during seal season, Sandy was not a discriminating hunter.

And she still had not reappeared on sonar.

That meant one of two things. Either she had left the area... or else she had picked a target and gone deep.

As Amber regarded the black surface, she became aware of a physical unwillingness to go back in. It was a bizarre feeling really, almost like a physical weight. It was the mind and body at odds, sort of like when the wake-up alarm instructs your mind to force your exhausted, sleepy body out of bed.

She'd let that image get into her head – Sandy ascending smoothly and powerfully out of the dark water – and Amber suddenly realized she was in danger of forfeiting the race. The Surfer Dude had frozen the day before. And it was in the boat that it had happened; your body simply wouldn't let you leave safety.

It would, Amber realized, be so easy to just sit there and let her time run out. She sat up abruptly, thinking that if she didn't get back in soon, she might not be able to at all. Her mind was tough and could force her into anything. The shark image was a primal one, however, and it invoked a forgotten, involuntary survival mode, built into the behavior system before the human mind was added to fuck things up.

There were three more minutes left in her second Out. Ahead, Stephen was nearing the end of his own first turn. He was still standing and scanning, taking a last look around. He waved at Amber.

"Ladies first," Stephen said over the radio.

He *was* waiting her out. God damn it.

No matter, she decided, she had to go in now anyway. She could feel the lethargy slipping insidiously into her veins. It wasn't fatigue; it was the weakening desire to give up. Going tharn. Amber resisted it all, stepping one foot up on the boat's edge.

Leprechaun tapped his watch, indicating she still had time left. Amber shook her head, taking a breath, bracing for the hateful, cold grab of the ocean. She took one last scan of the surface. Then she heard Stephen's voice over the radio again.

"Ah, what the hell," he said.

A hundred yards ahead, Dreyfuss reentered the water with a splash.

And almost immediately, he was hit.

Amber had a good clear view. Sandy hit Stephen from below, catching him full-on the moment he touched the water. It was a textbook attack, with the torpedo-like body blasting completely clear of the surface.

Stephen's body was torn cleanly in two, with part of his upper torso spinning off like a rag doll, landing, floating on the ocean surface. A moment later, the conical snout reappeared, snapping the flotsam up like goldfish flakes.

Leprechaun had gotten the whole thing on camera with his zoom lens. "That was a good one," he said. He turned to Amber. "There's a break for you, darlin'."

Tattoo suddenly turned the guard boat hard right. Far in the distance, Kurt's boat did likewise. An attack was a free Out and an automatic relocation a safe but equal distance away. That was good because an attack, on human or seal, often brought other sharks scouting.

Amber sat quietly in her boat, not reacting – at least not visibly. Stephen was the first elimination she had ever seen in person. Leprechaun kept the camera on her – Mason liked reaction shots. But he soon sat the camcorder down, disappointed; on the surface, at least, Amber was as distant and defiant as ever.

There was a real battle going on inside her, however. Her mind, her toughness, which had forced her along this far, found itself being assailed by the constant blaring, unarguable image of Stephen Dreyfuss' spinning rag doll form. It was that old recurring dream of being eaten. He had been snapped up from below like a guppy.

Seagulls had gathered in the water and air on the site, attracted by bright clouds of blood in the water. The gulls would be disappointed, Amber thought. Stephen Dreyfuss was gone. His guard boat puttered around, filming.

Amber lurched as Tattoo turned the boat to a stop. Leprechaun smiled again, still enjoying his job too much. "You're up, darlin'," he said.

Ahead, Kurt's boat spun to a stop as well. She could see Kurt standing, staring back at them. Kurt still had Outs to spare. He was waiting on her. Amber stared down at the water.

She was still staring when the Leprechaun informed her she'd just stepped over into her third Out. And counting.

Amber stood there as the minutes ticked. The war raged inside her head for the possession of her body.

Tattoo turned the boat in the opposite direction, back towards Mason's yacht. She would be losing distance now.

Far ahead, too far ahead, Kurt reentered the race with a quick efficient dive, resuming his easy broad stroke. He still had to finish to win. That was the rules. So would Amber, if Kurt were to be eliminated. Whoever was left would have to swim the last stage alone.

Perhaps that was what did it – the thought of swimming the stage alone. Odd, since that was what she would have prayed for… the only way she could win. It was, however, that very thought that decided it once and for all.

Her mind screamed defiance, raging inside her head, demanding that she get up and finish, commanding her inert flesh with accustomed authority, accepting no refusal.

Nevertheless, Amber still sat there quietly as Leprechaun counted down the minutes and seconds until her last Out was over. Tattoo gunned the boat back towards Mason's yacht. If she didn't reenter the race before they got there, she would be eliminated.

She thought for a moment of the Surfer Dude and the screams she had thought she heard the night before.

But still she sat, arm circled around her knees, as the guard-boat left the race behind. For Amber, the Contest was over.

CHAPTER 13

Alex was standing on the top deck when the guard-boat arrived back at the yacht with Amber. The day was cloudy, depressing even, not good for sunbathing. Alex, however, preferred the deck to the main cabin as Mason had his video feed set up from the guard-boats' cameras. He was watching Stephen Dreyfuss' elimination. Over and over.

Mason's reactions to the video images were an unnerving thing to see. It reminded Alex of something she'd read about Ted Bundy when he was in prison. The local cops had broached Bundy, himself an accomplished murderer and rapist, consulting him like a real-life Hannibal Lector for help catching the Green River Killer. The investigators had brought a photograph of one of the victims from the crime scene and they said Bundy literally devoured the photograph with his eyes; absorbing the snapshot of the dead, mutilated girl as if it were "the most provocative bit of pornography."

That was how Mason looked as he played and replayed the bloody elimination.

Alex had risen, nauseated, feigning disinterest. She made casually for the stairs, hoping Mason wouldn't call her back. He sometimes did that when the elimination was a good one.

Or like last night.

It was all probably lucky for Amber, Alex thought; Mason was in a good mood. Amber might not find herself swimming with the sharks tonight for ditching the race. Alex stared down over the railing, watching as the guard-boat pulled up beside with Amber.

Amber, herself, looked quite subdued. There was none of the venomous eye contact from days before. She was humbled as Mason's Contest was likely to make you.

Mason himself remained below, not deigning to acknowledge Amber as she retired briefly to her quarters. She showed up a few minutes later, changed into dry clothes, with a packed knapsack.

Alex was surprised. Mason was just letting her leave. He never did that with quitters. He usually at least scared the shit out of them first. Nevertheless, Amber rejoined Tattoo and the Leprechaun in the guard-boat, and they sped quickly away towards shore. The boat quickly became indistinct in the hazy afternoon.

Mason remained below, and Alex heard him on the radio, asking the remaining guard-boats for news on Kurt's progress.

Alex knew what was coming next. Kurt was the last. Assuming he simply made it to the island, all he had to do was finish the stage tomorrow alive. That meant for all practical purposes, the race was over.

But once again, the Contest was Mason's Christmas. Or perhaps his New Year's party would be a better analogy. New Year's was a party. And when the party slows down, you simply spike the punch.

Alex, of course, had been through all this before. She knew what Mason had in mind.

CHAPTER 14

Kurt Wagner did not hurry – as far as the race was concerned, nothing had changed; he still had to finish alive. Finishing alive was the real trick. Therefore his stroke remained smooth, his pace unhurried. Just because his competitors had fallen did not guarantee him his prize.

He allowed nothing that had happened to affect his physical moves. That was the trained athlete in him – his body performed on its own. It was an ability he had trained to be innate with in him. It was the product of years of discipline, a power that had once been his pride - for a minute there, he really had been the best.

But being the best didn't matter much in this race. The sharks couldn't care less. And knowing this, Kurt focused pointedly on the task at hand, avoiding, above all, the image that had burned into his subconscious like a laser disc: the image of a sudden eruption of water and the bloody elimination of Stephen Dreyfuss. Kurt had kind of liked Dreyfuss – he was sort of like the smart but nerdy kid you remember from science class.

Stephen had been torn apart. The water fountaining around the leaping 5,000-pound fish had turned instantly red, clouding like ink. The splash as the attacking Carcharodon's body crashed back down, was clouded with the greater portion of Dreyfuss' life-blood.

For Kurt the simple act of thinking around that image seemed to create a mental silhouette around it, in effect only clarifying it in his mind. The simple effort of trying to remove it turned the image into a fixture in his mind, impossible to remove once established. This, Kurt thought, was why Amber had quit. It was why he, himself, wanted to quit now.

Partly why. Not all.

Kurt glanced up at the guard-boat trolling along behind him. He'd almost forgotten they were there. Not much point to remembering – he had absolutely no belief they would do anything more than film it, should a shark suddenly take an interest in him.

The guards today were the Cyborg and Blackbeard, both of whom he'd been pestering with his penlight the night before.

He shouldn't have done that, Kurt decided. Not that he cared the slightest about the two mercs, but because it brought into focus another fixture he had tried to hide from in his mind. It was this fixture that dominated all his thoughts, simply by their conscious absence; it was not his career, or anything to do with sharks, nor the press or Mason himself – the dark spot in his mind was for his wife, Anna. The penlight he had shined into his subhuman guards' eyes had been a gift from his wife – a thoughtless, thoughtful, I-got-you-something-type gift, an Olympic souvenir, bought the day before she'd discovered she had cancer. Two weeks before the end of her life.

Kurt had been playing with the light in her eyes that night, teasing her, actually making her mad. They'd had their last fight because of it. It was a good strong light too, with a clear-beam, waterproof, and the damn batteries seemed to last forever. Kurt had worn it like an albatross ever since.

Perhaps it was the long-suffered weight of that albatross that was the rest of the reason Kurt found himself wanting to quit. The attack had been bad, certainly, and yes, it had rattled him – yes, the image was burned like a negative on the modem screen of his brain and would probably remain so for life – but in truth, Kurt's desire to quit had nothing to do with any of that. It had nothing to do with losing his nerve or with fear. It was more a sense of foolishness. Foolishness and waste.

Steven Dreyfuss had been a Joe-blow kind of guy – a nice guy with a spark of intelligence that had separated him. And Kurt was sure that the spectrum of problems that had brought him into Mason's Contest had seemed bad enough when viewed within the framework of his own life. In retrospect, however, they hadn't been so hard to solve after all. And Kurt would be willing to bet that Dreyfuss, if asked, would have kept the problems over the solution. It maybe would have been worth it to try another way first.

It made Kurt wonder why he was still here – why he had continued on after Amber, and the Surfer Dude before her, had given up.

Certainly, his competitive background contributed; all athletics depended as much on mental discipline as physical abilities – at least at the top levels – and Kurt had set his mind to the task at hand. He had started it and he would by-God finish it.

There was also the supporting fact that Amber's were not the only ears sharp enough to have caught those distant screams the night before. Mason didn't like quitters.

These were *reasons*, of course… but not *the* reason. The truth was Kurt remained swimming because of that same albatross penlight.

The albatross was a punishment he'd imposed upon himself. He was punishing himself for everything that had happened after Anna had died – he was punishing himself for *letting* her die; he should have simply *willed* it not to happen. And all his reckless, stupid behavior since was simply his small, mortal self, spitting tiny defiance into the eye of fate. But his presence in Mason's Contest was nothing but a petition for validation by that same fate – a judgment of his own worthiness to live while Anna had gone.

Except that now Kurt had come to realize that this Contest wasn't really like that at all. Colin Mason was nothing but a sick and depraved man – a rich noble who liked to watch people running from the lions. All serial-type murders were based on the killer's imposition of power over the victim. Colin Mason was no different. This Contest wasn't fate at all; fate is happenstance – the Contest was odds stacked in favor of the house.

Amber had been right. It was a set-up. It was a race the contestants were supposed to lose.

There was, however, not a hell of a lot Kurt could do about it now.

And since he was in it, he was *in* it. He had no choice but to see it through. He pushed all thoughts of Mason and the prize out of his head, along with any lingering thoughts of sharks, exploring seals, or tattered human debris flinging, spinning from a toothed maw like wet, bloody rags.

He thought of Anna and decided his time for mourning should be over. He made a promise to her and to himself that when this was all over, he would change his life on his own, prize or no prize.

Of course, he still had to live to see it done.

The shore was growing close now. Fighting the urge to hurry, Kurt knew he was nearing the end of the second stage. He could see the bonfire already prepared on the beach, along with three tents set up on the rocks. As he drew closer, he saw one of Mason's guards – it looked like Mercer himself – pulling down the first two tents. They would only be needing one tonight.

Kurt had reached the outcropping of reefs that circled the beach, and took a moment to look around before swimming past. This was traditionally one of the danger spots; sharks frequently hit seals from the deep drop-offs beyond. It was the head of steam from the deep water that produced the spectacular Air-Jaws footage that had highlighted both Dreyfuss' and Mason's videos alike. The reef itself provided its own dangers as well, with its rocks being quite sharp; it was pretty hairy going over some of these barnacle-encrusted edges when the sea was rough. Once you passed, however, it was a short, straight shot to the beach.

Kurt made it past the reefs unscathed and unmolested, stroking smoothly and easily, still resisting the urge to hurry the last hundred yards to the beach. Mercer was standing there waiting as Kurt stumbled out of the surf a few minutes later, plopping exhausted – too exhausted – onto a big log in front of the fire.

The weariness that sank into Kurt's bones was more than the day's swim should have warranted. Psychologically, he was growing weak. Mason's mind game was working. Kurt lay there, ignoring Mercer as he radioed in Kurt's finish time back to Mason. He also eschewed the tent, stretching out on the dried, sun-warmed log, grateful for just the simple, solid feel of dry land. Kurt shut his eyes, absorbing the warmth of the fire on his ocean-chilled skin, doing his best to exist in the here and now, pushing from his mind especially any thoughts of the water, or the third stage that would come on the morrow – the third stage which he would be swimming alone.

The roll of the ocean was hypnotic and, although he hadn't meant to, Kurt must have slept for a time. When he awoke, sudden and chilled, the sky had grown dark.

Mason was sitting there with him, staring at him over the fire.

CHAPTER 15

"I'll give you ten million if you do it tonight," Mason said.

Kurt stared back, momentarily disoriented and dozy. It took a moment to process Mason's words. When they did finally compute, however, Kurt came fully awake and aware. The early evening chill caused a rush of goose-flesh and Kurt found himself glancing furtively out at the ocean – the cooling air was misty with the surf, a clammy sensation on the skin, not unlike the anticipatory twist of dread in his gut.

The ocean always sounded louder at night. More powerful. You were aware of it as a force of nature.

Kurt regarded Mason with steady eyes. "Are you trying to kill me, Mr. Mason?" he asked.

Mason's smile was the same, slow, Cheshire-cat grin that he used when Kurt had been first recruited. The flame light turned it into a shark-like grimace. Kurt was uneasy at the sight of that smile, but not yet afraid – Mercer still stood at a distance, allowing Mason the privacy for business dealings. That was encouraging – if nothing else, Mason seemed to respect his own rules as far as the Contest was concerned.

Nevertheless, the sight of the two of them, Mason with his *Jaws*-poster grin and Mercer skulking in the background, caused Kurt to reflect how isolated they were out here. Literally anything could happen to a person this far from the eyes of the world. And the scariest part was that you didn't have to go far to get this lost – San Francisco's coast remained a glow of smog-sky on the east horizon.

"Ten million," Mason said again. "No tricks. You do the final stage tonight and it's yours."

Kurt looked at him steadily and asked again: "Are you trying to kill me?"

Mason's eyes became slits like that same Cheshire cat.

"I've always been trying to kill you, Mr. Wagner," Mason said. "The price of your life just suddenly became worth more."

"Why?" Kurt asked.

Mason sighed, leaning back in his wheelchair, casting his gaze up at the stars. For a moment he looked older, almost kindly, the portrait of a wistful, older man, aged in his heart beyond his years. "Why?" Mason echoed softly. "Why, Mr. Wagner?" He turned his eyes back from the stars, meeting Kurt's with unaffected and simple earnest. "The reason is because I enjoy few things in life these days. This Contest is one. In fact, it is *the* one." He shrugged. "This year's is all but over."

The wistful expression vanished, replaced once again by the shark-like grin.

"It needs something to spice it up," Mason said.

A long moment of silence followed. Kurt waited but Mason had fallen silent, apparently because all sales really convince themselves. Mason had put his deal on the table. Now the two of them studied each other while Kurt considered.

After several minutes of silence, Mason said, "You don't have to decide right now." He checked his watch. "It's only a little after eight o'clock. Take another two hours to consider it. Rest up. We'll call the start time ten-thirty pm."

"Ten million?" Kurt said, reflectively. The number was not unattractive… and of course, he had to do the race anyway.

"Ten million," Mason agreed. "If you make it, I'll give it to you right there on the boat."

Kurt frowned. "You keep that much on the boat? With all these mercs around?" He shook his head. "That seems a bit risky to me."

Mason's grin became disarming. "Don't worry about me, Mr. Wagner," he said. "I always keep my most trusted guard close at hand."

Kurt glanced up at the foreboding presence of Mercer, who was hugging the shadows along the perimeter of the clearing. Mercer's metal-plate eyes reflected the light like a dog's. Kurt turned back to Mason.

"What about all those party girls?" Kurt said, "Or that little blond you keep on the boat – I'd watch that one if I were you."

Mason made a dismissive wave of his hand. He turned his wheelchair on its heel, rolling it roughly over the rocks. Mercer stepped up quickly behind him, pushing him back towards the guard-boat. Mason smiled at Kurt over his shoulder.

"I'll give you 'till ten o'clock," Mason said. "Consider it well, Mr. Wagner. Ten million."

Mason raised his hand and Mercer paused, turning the chair back for a moment. Mason was at the edge of the light and the Cheshire cat had faded away – only the smile remained. Mason's voice was as disembodied as a ghost's.

"Ten million to swim it tonight – it could all be over in a few short hours, saving you the waiting tonight.

"And when you think about it," the spectral voice continued, beckoning, "it's the best deal you could make. Carcharodons don't hunt at night. They like surface prey. And at night the surface is invisible."

Then the conversational voice dropped to a sinister whisper. Kurt felt the sting of goose-flesh on his arms once again.

"Of course, the sharks are still there," Mason said, "they're always there and they never sleep... and just think what it will be like out there. Alone. In the dark."

Mason checked his watch again.

"'Till ten o'clock, Mr. Wagner," he said.

Kurt stared back quietly as Mercer turned Mason back around, steering him towards the boat over the rough rocks. Mason, perhaps revealing a pretense for Kurt's benefit, hopped out of his wheelchair, springing athletically on his one good leg, vaulting easily into the guard-boat. He winked at Kurt as Mercer folded the wheelchair and joined him aboard.

The boat's engine roared to life and Mercer steered the boat away from shore, angling towards the distant lights of Mason's yacht. Kurt watched them go. He glanced over down the beach where waited the Cyborg and Blackbeard, with their own guard-boat standing by. The two mercs sat impassively in the dark, shadows among the rocks.

Kurt turned his attention to the ocean.

Mason had been right, Kurt thought; it would be safer to swim at night. He had also been right when he thought to imagine what it might be like out there in the dark.

Kurt considered. He rose from the log, walking down the beach to where the tide rolled in. He stretched his limbs experimentally; they were tired, but he could swim at a slow jog for hours. Physically, he knew he could do it without a hitch.

He heard Mason's voice: "In a few short hours it could all be over."

With ten million dollars on top of that.

And one other thing Mason said had been true – it would save him the night of waiting. The growing, gnawing fear in his gut would be done. One way or another it would end – sooner rather than later.

He thought about the promise he had made to himself and to his wife tonight, pulling out his penlight and flashing it out onto the ocean. He sat contemplatively like that for the next two hours, flicking the light on and off reflectively, blinking the light like a message in Morse, as if he was seeking advice from the ocean itself. His decision, however, was made fairly early on. The rest of the time was just waiting for ten o'clock to roll around.

When it did, Kurt rose and walked out into the surf.

CHAPTER 16

The sharks were out there waiting. Kurt could *feel* them – great dark shapes, rendered invisible by the nightfall, hidden, if only for the moment. If they chose to take him, there would not even be the warning of the circling fin; all they had was the sonar, which until now had not been exactly foolproof. Even now, Kurt could hear the sonar warning beeps from the guard-boat – registering nothing and everything, like a radar detector in the city.

So far, there was nothing substantial. Kurt, however, took uncomfortable note of the full moon.

Except for the moon, the night was purest black. Kurt could hear the guard-boat trolling along behind him, but couldn't see it; the boat was running with no lights, cameras off, not even trusting infrared against the Carcharodons' senses. They spared Kurt the spotlight. A spotlight would have been like putting a target over his head.

He had not, however, considered the full moon, which functioned much the same way. Big and full, it made him more visible on this night over all others.

Kurt wondered if Mason planned things like that.

It was almost easier to believe that than the possibility that chance might simply be working against him. There was, for example, the fact that the ocean seemed to have gotten a hell of a lot colder now that night had fallen. In the reference section of his brain, where he kept his book-learning, Kurt knew that the ocean's temperature barely changed with the seasons, let alone day and night. His nerves however, told him with utter authority that that was purest bullshit, because Kurt was freezing his ass off. Maybe it was the lack of sun on his exposed back and shoulders that made the difference, but it was colder now that the sun had fallen. He was also aware of a breeze that he must not have noticed before – the air itself had gone cold with nothing on either side but the icy ocean or the sunless sky. The nervous jitters running up and down his spine didn't help.

Mason was getting his money's worth tonight; although Kurt's professional crawl stroke revealed none of it, Kurt was fighting a steady pump of adrenaline, injected into his system with each succeeding heartbeat. His nerves were jittering as with an overdose of caffeine tablets; his breathing came in quick gasps that he forced into long rhythmic inhales, timed with his swimming stroke. But there was an icy edge to his movements that was not just the cold water.

Tonight, more than at any point in the race so far – in fact probably more than at any time of his life – Kurt was afraid.

In fact, he was terrified. Fear couldn't possibly describe the freezing feeling that tightened up his gut. It rattled his mental focus as well, like a stuttering mouse pad; Kurt wasn't sure if it was the sharks or Mason's head games finally getting to him, but he found his self-control slipping by degrees. It was growing worse instead of better, as if instead of racing to safety, he was headed ever closer to some bad end.

Mason might not be aware of it, but there was a new race on, Kurt thought; the question was now whether or not he could finish before he totally lost it. In an intellectual way, his mind – taking stock of the enemy – was surprised that it would be a near thing. His body threatened to act on its own.

Kurt brought all his mental weapons to bear, however, calling up images of Anna, the Olympics, the cancer, and all of it. He remembered the night he'd been awarded Olympic Gold and the night that had followed with his wife. He brought up the anger of her sickness, and the betrayal when the powers-that-be stripped him of the medal that he had spent a lifetime of discipline in order to earn.

A lifetime of discipline provided inertia – it had been training for more than just racing. It was supposed to have brought him success and fortune, liberty and happiness, just like the Document says. There had been much sacrifice along the way, but in the end, he had done it all, just like he was supposed to. He had done everything and more than anybody could ever have expected, and he had pulled it off. He had won. He'd made it. That had been right before he had learned that life could up and fuck you over anyway.

The glow of anger fanned brighter. It even helped a little – even if a goodly portion of that anger might remain directed at himself. He'd taken a few bad breaks – he'd had no control over that – but then, without Anna to prop him up, he had given up on life. Had he really expected life to be easy once he got to the top? He guessed he had. His presence in this race was the final evidence of his own cop out.

But he could still come out all right. Better than all right, if he made it. All he had to do was endure a little more, enduring it like he had endured the endless hours of training, or the even more endless hours in the days following Anna's cancer.

You just shut it off, he thought, until it's over or goes away. Grief was no different than terror; it was all in your mind. Therefore, you had to hide from it in your body, and let your mind fade away. Kurt did just that. His stroke alternated between the breast and crawl stroke, resting different muscles alternately, staying economical and minimizing movement. He ignored his own blindness, and streaked through the water like a skipping stone.

Or a tasty little seal.

It occurred to Kurt to wonder if sharks could sense fear like dogs – if perhaps the sheer psychic shrillness of panic was audible to the Carcharodons' arsenal of sensory organs. A fish in distress, sick or injured, made those types of jerky movements associated with panic – movements that sent vibrations through the water like sound. Wasn't it possible the smallest tremor of terror in Kurt's own movements might do the same?

Everyone had gotten a good laugh at Amber's expense that afternoon – all those circling seals. The mercs had obviously seen that sort of thing before. But if a seal came upon Kurt now, he would scream like Amber had. He would scream and choke on the salt water. He would gag and choke, and maybe drown, and the water would taste like blood.

Seawater *was* like blood, almost identical to plasma – it was the lifeblood of the earth. All that was missing from its taste was that slightly metallic twang of whole blood. In that sense, Kurt was the foreign element in the earth's bloodstream. The sharks would be considered Great White corpuscles.

As if on cue, the sonar on the boat beeped, one solid note, and fell silent.

Kurt froze in the water - there had been several minor chirps and quips from the sonar box, but this one was a solid beep. On the guard-boat, the Cyborg fiddled with his instruments. "Nothing else," he said. "It didn't sound organic, though. It sounded like metal. Maybe it's something in the rocks."

Of course, Kurt knew that the water in which he currently found himself had dropped off quite deeply for a number of miles now, ever since the island's circling reef.

For a moment, the war was nearly lost. Kurt's body very nearly rebelled, exhorting, *demanding*, that he leave the water, take an Out, that he quit even. That deeper, more primitive survival instinct actually tried to mutiny for control and his body jerked involuntarily towards the guard-boat's railing with one hand.

Jerkily, just like a wounded fish.

But Kurt held back. He treaded water and waited on the sonar. He knew if he got out now the matter would be settled – he would never get back in. It was as simple as that. And after several long minutes of silence from the sonar, there was no choice but to go on; Kurt leaned back into his stroke and resumed the race.

The full moon had reached its zenith in the sky, and Kurt had been swimming for over two hours, when he tasted the tangy, metallic twang on his lips.

And somehow he knew what he would find when he pulled the penlight from his belt and switched it on.

The water around him glowed red in the beam of the penlight. The ocean was clouded with blood.

For a moment, he was nearly awestruck with horror. And for a split second, he thought maybe he'd been bit, just like the girl in *Jaws*, who feels down for her leg only to find that it's not there. Kurt's own legs were both there, however, and when his paralysis finally broke, they began kicking vigorously, splashing like an amateur. He swallowed water and blood and the very thought made him gag and choke.

Then he recognized another taste, and a stench, and he understood.

It was chum. He was swimming in a fucking chum-slick – Mason was trying to fuck him after all.

And in that very moment, Kurt was certain he felt the displaced water as something passed unseen below.

Fuck this, he thought. *His* race was over.

"Hey!" he shouted at the mercs, "Hey, you assholes! Get me out of here!" He lurched in the direction of the guard-boat.

The spotlight suddenly appeared blindingly in the dark. The water around him was clouded red and oily with fish guts. Fucking Mason was trying to kill him. Kurt swam frantically for the light, swearing a curse on Mason and his entire fucking clan, and God help the son of a bitch if Kurt lived to face him down.

The spotlight had found him and Kurt swam for it blindly.

A second later there came a soft, spitting sound from somewhere behind. This was followed by a heavy grunt, like a man who has taken a blow to the chest. There was a thump in the guard-boat and the spotlight spun crazily. Then there was the sound of a heavy splash and darkness again.

A voice spoke out, clearly Blackbeard's, gruff and alarmed: "What the fuc-kuuhhhhh!?"

The voice was interrupted by another spitting sound, followed by another splash.

Then silence.

Blind in the dark Kurt groped for the boat. His mind was racing – what the hell was going on? – but his body had taken over and was going to by-God get him the fuck out of this ocean. His floundering hands caught hold of something large in the water in front of him. Momentary panic was replaced with sudden, cold dread when he realized it was not a shark but a body. The texture of facial hair under Kurt's hand identified it as Blackbeard. A flash from the penlight revealed a bullet hole shot neatly through the forehead. Most of the back of the head was missing.

That was when Kurt's control finally snapped. He lunged in the dark for the guard-boat. It was close ahead and he banged his hand painfully on the metal railing. Nevertheless, he latched on like a vice, hauling himself up and out of the water in a single movement, nearly capsizing the fourteen-foot boat. He struggled to steady himself in the dark, coughing up bloody water and actually felt better for one absurd moment, as if he had found some sort of sanctuary.

Then there was another spitting sound.

It felt like something had hit him in the chest. He tried to breathe but found that he could not.

There was a second spitting sound a moment later and Kurt's brains were blown out one side of his head. His world shut off like a light.

Mason's Contest had now ended for Kurt too.

He toppled limply backwards out of the boat. In the water below came the first curious browsing of the sharks.

CHAPTER 17

Mason sat in the dark, up on the top deck of his yacht, watching for anything that might happen to materialize out on the darkened ocean. He kept the boat lights off in deference to the swimmer, keeping true to his word, and true to the rules of the Contest; he relied on the guard-boats to keep the swimmer on course, the finish line being this very boat.

None of his guards had radioed within the last hour. He knew something was wrong – in fact, he had known for some time – but he was still fuzzy on some of the details. But this was obviously it.

He had left Alex asleep upstairs and he was otherwise alone on the boat. At End-Game, he always had no more guards than necessary to man the boats. Everyone else, he sent all the way back to shore – all to be checked in and verified at his house. There was a lot of money sitting around on this particular yacht.

But it seemed things were now coming down to the principals – just like it always did.

Mercer he had sent to observe from a distance, just to keep an eye on things - Mercer hadn't checked in either.

Mason sighed; he had the feeling that, one way or another, this year's Contest was over.

He made his way down the steep stairway to the main deck, hopping easily on his one foot, carrying his wheelchair in one hand, gripping the rail with the other. Once down, he plopped back into the padded chair and rolled over to the railing. He took a breath of ocean and recognized the pungent stench of chum.

Mason flicked on the underwater lights and his nostrils were confirmed. The water was clouded red with blood and fish guts. Someone had run a chum slick all around the boat.

And in the dim illumination of the boat lights, a faint shadow flickered past in the water beneath, just beyond the reach of sight.

One of his mercs had thought it was funny during the fourth year of the Contest to chum one of the stages of the race. Mason had the man's own friends turn *him* into chum the next day, one piece at a time, alive through all but the most extreme stages. All on film of course.

Someone was almost suicidally confident, Mason decided. And as he happened to catch another flicker of movement, this one from the main cabin, he had a pretty good idea who.

Mason wheeled his way inside.

Alex was on the floor in front of his safe, working the combination to the light of the computer screen on his desk. Mason noticed his own personal screen had been raised up. Alex glanced up at him as he came in. Their eyes locked for a fraction of a second. Alex's eyes carried a glint of defiance she had never quite dared before.

She turned her attention pointedly back to the safe, deliberately turning the last number in the combination with a slow 'click.'

Inside was the million dollars of cash Mason had promised to the winner. Alex reached in and pulled out the cash like winnings in Vegas. She began packing the money into a good-sized duffel.

Mason sat quietly until she finished; she zipped the bag and looked up at him, raising a small pistol in one hand and pointing it at Mason.

And Mason smiled.

CHAPTER 18

Alex leveled the gun at Mason's forehead, demonstrating competence in her handling. She didn't think Mason would try to test her – he knew enough about her to know she wouldn't bluff. Alex had done plenty of target-shooting with an old hunter/military boyfriend and, while she'd never shot at a man, she believed Mason knew she could put it right between his eyes if she wanted.

His smile, however, was disconcerting.

She rose from the floor, holding the gun steady, tossing the duffel over one shoulder, leaning from its weight, and she sat down in front of Mason's computer – which Mason had, by satellite, hooked into almost all his accounts. He sometimes spent months at sea.

The cash in the duffel was just traveling money. Alex had much larger stakes in mind.

She had been around for a while now, long enough to know how Mason got things done. In the case of the Contest, it was to Alex's benefit that Mason was so ritualized. In the three years Alex had been with him, Mason had raised the stakes to the final contestants three separate times. He kept his accounts open, sometimes depositing the contestants' winnings directly – he owned several banks and all he really needed was their account number.

It was also a good way to demonstrate his absolute control over the world and all things if any of his Survivor's Club should decide to talk about the race.

Alex had known Mason's access codes for most of his big accounts for almost a year now. Of course, there had been other things to arrange – things that Mason's Contest neatly dovetailed.

When Mason walked in on her, Alex had already done most of the work; she'd simply emptied Mason's accounts into her own – all off shore of course; it had taken her less than twenty minutes. That satellite bill was worth every penny.

Mason, however, was still smiling. And when he spoke, his tone was amused – as if catching his teenaged daughter sneaking in after curfew.

"So," he said, "we've got our hand in the cookie-jar, do we?"

Alex leveled the gun and said nothing. Mason shook his head sadly. "Alex. My dear Alex – after all I've done for you."

An odd crook appeared in Alex's brow – it meant she was repressing.

In her head was conjured up an image of endless nights of bondage and crazy snuff-porn and shark films. Alex found she enjoyed the sight of Mason's face now that it was viewed down the barrel of her pistol. It was wonderful that he was every bit as scummy as she wanted him to be.

"So what happens now?" Mason asked. "Are you really prepared to shoot me?"

"If I have to," Alex said.

"You know how I work," Mason said. "I always keep my most trusted guard close at hand on the last night of the race."

"But he's out on the water now, isn't he?" Alex reminded him. "Right where you sent him."

But even at that moment, there came the sound of a boat engine. From the direction of the sound, a spotlight suddenly switched on. The beam of light passed through the windows of the main cabin. The engine was growing closer.

Mason raised amused eyebrows. "You should probably hurry up and shoot," he said.

"Get outside," Alex said, moving up warily behind him – not too close, though. She knew full well how strong he was and how fast he could be on top of her. It hadn't happened often – just enough for her to know it. Mason's back was a tempting target as he rolled himself casually out the door.

Mercer was climbing aboard. He looked up and saw the two of them, Alex with her gun, and he froze.

Mason watched him expectantly. "Well, Mr. Mercer, what do I pay you for?"

Mercer turned slowly in Alex' direction. Alex raised the gun from Mason to Mercer. For all the good it would have done – Mercer moved in three quick steps, and Alex felt his hands upon her before she was even aware he'd started to move. It was all done so matter-of-fact; it was what made Mercer so damned frightening. Alex actually froze up, and suddenly Mercer's hand was on her wrist, bending her little .22 out of her hand and dropping it into his own.

"Cute," Mercer said, stuffing it into his pocket. From his holster he pulled out his own 475 Linebaugh, a big-ass, five-shot, monster revolver – the gun Dirty Harry would be shooting today.

Mason couldn't help it: "I guess it is the size of your gun that matters."

Alex stared up into Mason's steely eyes… and smiled.

Mercer cocked the pistol, turned and leveled it at Colin Mason. Alex curled herself up around Mercer's waist like a cat, her hands exploring. Mercer's own free hand rose up Alex's thigh. The gun was dead steady, aimed at Mason's face.

Mason's face grew long. "Et tu?" he said, sadly.

"I'm sorry, sir," Mercer said.

"No, Roland," Mason said, letting out a deep sigh. "I'm sorry. We've been together a long time. But I guess that money certainly does sing a swan song – and it's even sweeter when a lady-swan sings it." Mason's sad smile became genuinely regretful. "Don't worry. I understand. You're a merc, after all. And a paycheck is a paycheck."

Mason shrugged and clapped his hands. "So," he said brightly, "what happens now?"

Mercer frowned. He stepped up behind Mason's chair like he'd done a thousand times before, only now he had his gun pressed against the back of Mason's head. Mercer exchanged a glance with Alex.

Alex cut her eyes over the side. Mercer nodded and began wheeling Mason's chair towards the railing.

Mason nodded approvingly. "Ah yes. The sharks. How appropriate." And, as his chair was pushed towards the edge, Mason caught a view of the guard-boat and the bucket of chum Mercer had loaded aboard. Mason's eyes turned to Alex.

"So," he said, "it was you pulling the strings all along." He nodded over his shoulder at Mercer. "Have him chum the water, riling up the sharks and eliminating the swimmer, kill the guards dumping them into a feeding area." Mason smiled at Alex like a proud teacher. "I'm impressed. You're a real learner."

Alex stared back uncertainly and suddenly Mason's eyes grew darker. The smile grew traditionally predatory, and Alex found herself chilled.

"I'll always remember you like you were last night," Mason said, his voice barely a whisper.

Alex's repressive crook appeared again in her brow. She shivered, unable to keep the image of the previous night away.

It would be the last time, she assured herself.

In the water something snapped at a medium-sized, floating piece of chum. Alex nodded to Mercer.

This was the part she'd always hid from in her mind. Alex didn't think she could actually kill a person - but she could perhaps stand by and watch it done.

It wasn't like you could call Colin Mason a *person.*

And of course, it was Mercer who had killed all the others, who had chummed the water and shot the guards. But that was what he did, so that was okay. In fact, Mercer himself would probably wind up having an accident of his own not far down the line.

Mercer had pushed Mason's chair up against the railing. He would have to lift him physically out of his chair in order to pitch him over. Mercer glanced over at Alex. "Think we should shoot him first?"

Alex considered, then turned away as if bored. "That's really more your end of it, dear. You decide. If you think it would be more *merciful*..."

Mercer looked down at Mason who was still smiling gently. "I worked for you for a long time, sir," Mercer said. He stepped back, aiming the pistol professionally between the eyes. His finger teased on the trigger... and then he dropped the hammer back down and the gun fell to his side. "A long time," Mercer said, "and allow me to say, sir, you are one *sick* fuck." He holstered his side arm and nodded at Alex again. "I say we let him swim for it."

Alex smiled. "Whatever you think is best."

Mercer turned back to Mason and for the first time the hint of a smile touched his cyborg-features. Mason looked back at him, shaking his head sadly.

"You seem to forget, Mr. Mercer," Mason said, "how I do things. I said I keep my most trusted guard close." The shark smile returned. "I never said it was you."

In the shadows of the cabin behind them, just over Mercer's shoulder, there was a blur of movement.

There was a sudden electric flash and Mercer's eyes flew open, seeming to actually shoot sparks themselves. There was a sound like a blown circuit breaker and Mercer's body went bolt-rigid. The ozone-sulfurous smell was foul on the salt air.

Mercer dropped bonelessly to the deck.

Standing in the shadows, holding one of Mason's patented Shark Sticks, was Amber.

Mercer, Alex suddenly realized, had taken her own gun – Amber was, even at that moment, removing the baby .22 from

Mercer's pocket, relieving him also of his holstered .475. Amber smiled at the little .22 and stuffed it in her pocket.

Even in her shock, Alex took a moment to gawk at Amber's new dress code. In days before Amber had looked like a girl that might have grown up on farms, or perhaps an army base. Tonight was more the look you got living in a high-class Vegas brothel; the trend was strictly leather and lace.

The tough-breaks country girl had absorbed a street sophistication that enjoyed the night side of life completely and utterly. The striking green eyes had been looking into the dark for far too long.

Amber slipped up behind Mason's chair, rubbing the upper swell of her breast, nearly exposed in the low cut, dominatrix-style brazier, against the rough skin of his face. She licked her lips lusciously as she eyed Alex up and down.

A purring tiger might look something like Colin Mason did at just that moment. Alex herself was suddenly feeling a lot like a limping antelope.

Not having any better ideas, she simply asked, "Mason, who the hell is this bitch?"

Amber slowly raised the .475. Mason patted her hand. "Now, now," he said. He smiled at Alex. "Amber here is a very special contestant. You see, she and I go way back."

Amber rubbed her breasts over Mason's shoulder. The barrel of the heavy revolver was stork steady, aimed directly between Alex's eyes.

"You see," Mason said, "the story she told back on the beach was only half-true." He touched an aside to Amber: "By the way, dear," he said to her, "you were great – I got the whole thing on tape. Hilarious."

Amber eyed Alex contemplatively, the aim of the gun dropping to her chest.

"It was actually Amber herself who had the mob debt," Mason explained. "Not her poor brother. But the mob did kill him for it. That part was true."

Amber's eyes betrayed no emotion, just half-spacey concentration on her aim.

"When I met her," Mason said, "she was working off the rest of her debt as a high-priced call girl. In fact," he said, grinning, "it was in this very capacity that I met her, nearly twelve years ago."

Amber smiled. "And I fucked him so good, he never forgot me."

"Quite true," Mason agreed. "So along the way I bought out her contract. She belongs to me now. And when she came to me last year with this proposal – let her race for the million against another ten years' service – I said yes." Mason shrugged. "Neither of us really had anything to lose. Amber, for her part…" he patted her painted cheek, "… she really made most of her important decisions a long time ago."

Amber's eyes were shadowed in the dark, but they reflected the moon, and to Alex she looked like a fucking vampire.

Leaving Mason's shoulder, Amber bent behind his chair, grabbing Mercer by one paralyzed arm. With a better strength than Alex would have credited her with, she dragged his limp body over to the side and propped him up against the railing.

Alex could see awareness in Mercer's eyes – they rolled wildly, but his body was simply unable to respond.

Amber pulled the big-bladed knife from Mercer's belt. With a practiced cut and twist, she gutted him, spilling bloody ropes of intestines hanging out his belly.

The look in Mercer's eyes grew suddenly crazed.

Using the railing itself as a pivot point, Amber leveraged Mercer over the side like a heavy bag of laundry. He made an unremarkable-sounding splash. Amber's eyes turned to Alex.

"I've still got your money, Mason," Alex said quickly. "I emptied it all into my own accounts. If I disappear, you lose it for good."

Mason laughed heartily. "You mean that dummy program you've been playing with?" he asked. "The one I set up just for you? The one I set up right after my cameras caught you the first time you broke into my screen?"

Mason chuckled. "If you'd really succeeded in killing me, you would have had a big surprise wherever you tried to access those funds."

Alex's lips suddenly felt dry. She realized she'd had no secrets for months. Mason, unfortunately, still had.

Amber was walking towards her, the Linebaugh in one hand and Mercer's bloody knife in the other. The leather and lace, Vegas-hooker wardrobe was stained with the merc's blood. Amber walked the blade right up to Alex's throat, leaving a residue of red as she traced it down her bare skin.

The gun poked sharply in Alex's ribs; Amber nodded her towards the railing and Alex backed up until her back touched the top rail. Reaching up with the knife, Amber cut away the loose straps of Alex's robe, tossing it off her shoulders. Underneath, Alex wore her thong-bikini swimsuit, which she had never even gotten wet.

The night air was quite cold.

Mason was no longer smiling. "I'm really very disappointed in you, Alexis," he said. "You tried to kill me. You tried to rob me. You fucked my bodyguard. All of it – really out of line."

Amber traced Mercer's knife along Alex's back now. *"I'd fuck her,"* Amber said deliciously.

"I know you would, my dear," Mason said, shushing her.

Alex started to speak but Mason stopped her with an outstretched hand.

"You've done some very bad things, Miss Winters," Mason said. "Unforgivable things. But you know what really pisses me off?"

Alex did know. But Mason said it anyway.

"You fucked up my Contest."

And with that, Amber flipped Alex over the side.

The cold water arrested any potential scream, demanding instead a quick inhalation of air, upon which she immediately choked saltwater. She came up sputtering, spitting out the anchovy taste of ocean.

She could also taste the greasy residue of chum.

Mercer was floating close by. The sharks had yet to show any interest but he'd landed face first and it appeared he had drowned. Alex looked up at the boat. The lights were on below but the deck remained dark. Amber and Mason were shadows behind the rail and, in the dark, their eyes reflected the wave-glittered moonlight. Their eyes were as black and unblinking as those of the sharks themselves.

Something seemed to move at the perimeter of the light underneath the boat.

The current had started to pull her away and Alex instinctively moved towards the yacht. On board, she saw Amber raise the .475.

Alex sat like that for a moment, treading water in the dark as the boat drifted further away; she looked and saw the glowing shore of San Francisco – nearly twenty-seven miles away.

No chance, she thought. She would become lost and drown. Of course, she might make it to one of the islands.

But no – if she did that, they'd just chase her down and throw her right back in.

For that matter, she thought, might they not do the same thing if she actually made it to shore?

Alex considered. Of course, there was one thing she knew about Mason: he liked to feed people to his sharks – he enjoyed watching them die – but it was better if they had a fighting chance to win – a chance to get away. That was why they hadn't gutted her. They'd left her able to swim.

She could feel the shapes moving around her in the dark. As the light from the boat faded, she could no longer see anything at all; not Mercer's body, or anything except the circle of the moon – and perhaps the outline of one or two circling fins.

Alex couldn't tell whether or not one of them might have a crescent shaped bite taken out of it.

She was blind in the dark.

She began to swim.

THE END

CHECK OUT OTHER GREAT DEEP SEA THRILLERS

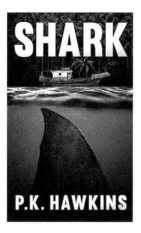

SHARK: INFESTED WATERS
by P.K. Hawkins

For Simon, the trip was supposed to be a once in a lifetime gift: a journey to the Amazon River Basin, the land that he had dreamed about visiting since he was a child. His enthusiasm for the trip may be tempered by the poor conditions of the boat and their captain leading the tour, but most of the tourists think they can look the other way on it. Except things go wrong quickly. After a horrific accident, Simon and the other tourists find themselves trapped on a tiny island in the middle of the river. It's the rainy season, and the river is rising. The island is surrounded by hungry bull sharks that won't let them swim away. And worst of all, the sharks might not be the only blood-thirsty killers among them. It was supposed to be the trip of a lifetime. Instead, they'll be lucky if they make it out with their lives at all.

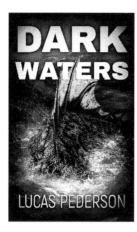

DARK WATERS
by Lucas Pederson

Jörmungandr is an ancient Norse sea monster. Thought to be purely a myth until a battleship is torn a part by one.

With his brother on that ship, former Navy Seal and deep-sea diver, Miles Raine, sets out on a personal vendetta against the creature and hopefully save his brother. Bringing with him his old Seal team, the Dagger Points, they embark on a mission that might very well be their last.

But what happens when the hunters become the hunted and the dark waters reveal more than a monster?

CHECK OUT OTHER GREAT
DEEP SEA THRILLERS

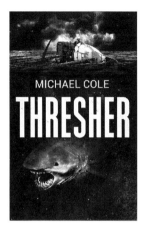

THRESHER
by Michael Cole

In the aftermath of a hurricane, a series of strange events plague the coastal waters off Florida. People go into the water and never return. Corpses of killer whales drift ashore, ravaged from enormous bite marks. A fishing trawler is found adrift, with a mysterious gash in its hull.

Transferred to the coastal town of Merit, police officer Leonard Riker uncovers the horrible reality of an enormous Thresher shark lurking off the coast. Forty feet in length, it has taken a territorial claim to the waters near the town harbor. Armed with three-inch teeth, a scythe-like caudal fin, and unmatched aggression, the beast seeks to kill anything sharing the waters.

THE GUILLOTINE
by Lucas Pederson

1,000 feet under the surface, Prehistoric Anthropologist, Ash Barrington, and his team are in the midst of a great archeological dig at the bottom of Lake Superior where they find a treasure trove of bones. Bones of dinosaurs that aren't supposed to be in this particular region. In their underwater facility, Infinity Moon, Ash and his team soon discover a series of underground tunnels. Upon exploring, they accidentally open an ice pocket, thawing the prehistoric creature trapped inside. Soon they are being attacked, the facility falling apart around them, by what Ash knows is a dunkleosteus and all those bones were from its prey. Now...Ash and his team are the prey and the creature will stop at nothing to get to them.

CHECK OUT OTHER GREAT DEEP SEA THRILLERS

THE BREACH
by Edward J. McFadden III

A Category 4 hurricane punched a quarter mile hole in Fire Island, exposing the Great South Bay to the ferocity of the Atlantic Ocean, and the current pulled something terrible through the new breach. A monstrosity of the past mixed with the present has been disturbed and it's found its way into the sheltered waters of Long Island's southern sea.

Nate Tanner lives in Stones Throw, Long Island. A disgraced SCPD detective lieutenant put out to pasture in the marine division because of his Navy background and experience with aquatic crime scenes, Tanner is assigned to hunt the creeper in the bay. But he and his team soon discover they're the ones being hunted.

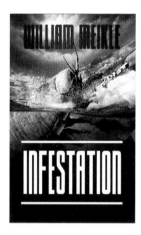

INFESTATION
by William Meikle

It was supposed to be a simple mission. A suspected Russian spy boat is in trouble in Canadian waters. Investigate and report are the orders.

But when Captain John Banks and his squad arrive, it is to find an empty vessel, and a scene of bloody mayhem.

Soon they are in a fight for their lives, for there are things in the icy seas off Baffin Island, scuttling, hungry things with a taste for human flesh.

They are swarming. And they are growing.

"Scotland's best Horror writer" - Ginger Nuts of Horror

"The premier storyteller of our time." - Famous Monsters of Filmland

Printed in Great Britain
by Amazon